## Here's what critics are saying about Stephanie Caffrey's books:

"A spectacular blend of hardboiled detective work and outrageously funny scenes. I can't imagine why anyone would want to miss out on a single book!"
—Fresh Fiction

"A great, breezy, fun read. Reminded me of Evanovich and Parker. Lots of sex and booze which is so Vegas."
—Chucktown Reader

"This is possibly the best first book of any series I have read. I am always looking for new authors and series, and this one is a true masterpiece. I can hardly wait for the next book."
—Mystery Lover

"This was such a refreshing, honest and out of the ordinary detective story. I think it was a cracking read and highly recommend it."
—Top 500 Amazon Reviewer (UK site)

D1608188

# BOOKS BY STEPHANIE CAFFREY

*Raven McShane Mysteries*:

Diva Las Vegas

Vegas Stripped

Royal Flush

Double Down

# DOUBLE DOWN

a Raven McShane mystery

Stephanie Caffrey

# DOUBLE DOWN

# CHAPTER ONE

---

Unlike most days, I had an appointment with a potential client. And he was late.

I didn't *do* late, myself. I was the kind of girl who got to a meeting early and then drove around the neighborhood for five minutes, watching the clock the whole time, and then appeared at exactly two minutes *after* the appointed hour, a self-imposed mini delay designed to avoid making me appear *too* eager, as though I had nothing better to do than show up exactly on time. Which, of course, was the truth. But being *actually* late, to the tune of ten or fifteen or even twenty minutes, was a concept so foreign, so abhorrent, that I considered it a personal insult, even though I knew deep down people's tardiness had nothing to do with little old me. They were just slackers, plain and simple.

Fifteen minutes. Of course, I had compounded the problem by obsessing about his lateness instead of actually doing anything productive in the meantime. But that's just how I was.

A knock came at the door, and then I heard it open. I sprung up from my chair and greeted my tardy visitor in the shabby high-ceilinged room that passed for my office lobby.

"Sorry I'm late," he huffed and puffed, a testament to the fact that my office was on the second floor, and he was overweight. "There was some kind of accident. The whole downtown is tied up."

"No problem," I said, lying through my teeth. "I was just finishing up a report."

He was still out of breath. "Dan Hartman," he breathed, holding out a sweaty palm.

I gripped it gingerly, stifling an *ewwwww*. "Let's sit," I said, leading him into my office. I was afraid the guy was going to drop dead on me.

Dan had a chubby face, bad skin, and the kind of beautiful wavy black hair you see in shampoo commercials, which made me wonder if God was playing a little joke by wasting that hair on a lardo like this. We made a little small talk, and then when his breathing had returned to its normal heavy wheeze, I got down to business.

"So you're a professional gambler," I said.

He winced. "I am a child of God, first. Second, a husband and father. Third, I coach my son's baseball team. Fourth, I'm a tenor in the choir. But yes, somewhere down on that list, I am a professional card player. It's not gambling, though," he said decidedly.

Now it was my turn to wince. In more than a decade of living in Las Vegas, I had met my share of folks who believed the time they spent in casinos wasn't gambling. They had a system, or had received a message from an alien, or believed in *something* that meant they had an edge on the house. Everyone *else* was gambling, but not them. It had grown tiresome long ago. My skepticism must have shown on my face.

Dan smiled. "I know that look. That's the look most of my family gives me when I explain it to them. *Yeah, right,* they're thinking. But I have evidence it works. You could check my bank account statements if you really want to."

I shook my head. "No. I'm sorry. I don't doubt you at all. It's nothing more than counting cards, right?"

He nodded. "Right. Blackjack is the only game in the casino where the past matters."

I wasn't following. "The past?"

Dan leaned forward in his seat, warming to the topic. "Yeah, the past. What I mean is, the cards that have already been played can tell you something about the cards that haven't been played yet. Get it?"

"Kind of," I lied.

"Let's say you're sitting there with six other people at your table, and every card dealt to the players is a five. What does that tell you?"

"That they each have ten," I said.

He chuckled. "Right. But what does it tell you about the cards that might be played next? What are the odds another five is going to come out of that shoe?"

I leaned back in my chair, which creaked under my own rapidly increasing weight. "It means it's very unlikely another five would come out. Almost all the fives have been dealt already."

Dan smiled. "Exactly. That's basically what we do."

"Except you're not counting fives," I said. "You're probably more interested in aces."

"Right. Aces and tens. Any ten or face card counts as ten. So if you keep track of how many have been played, you know the likelihood that another one will be played in the future. And that's how you make money."

I nodded, semi-intrigued. I had heard of card counting before—who hadn't—but never really thought about how it worked.

"So things are going well, but then…" I trailed off, leading him to the topic du jour.

"Yes," he said, "that's why I'm here. We've been on a losing streak. That happens all the time because you can't avoid the fact that there's always some luck involved, even when the odds are in your favor."

"But this time?" I prompted.

He sighed. "Let me put it this way. Mathematically, the chances we would be running this badly for so long are about one in five hundred. I'm not saying it's impossible. I'm just saying it would be hard to be *that* unlucky."

My mind made the logical leap. "So you're thinking someone's stealing from you? Someone on your team?"

Dan pursed his lips. "Unfortunately, yes, that's what I think. Or, at least, what I want to find out. That's where you come in."

I nodded, turning it over in my mind. "Let's back up a minute, though. How come you work in teams? Why not just play by yourself, and then you won't have to worry about this kind of thing?"

He leaned back in his chair. "Sometimes we do that. But if you have a team, you can exaggerate your advantages. If I'm sitting there all by myself betting ten bucks a hand, and then all of a sudden I start betting five hundred a hand, they're going to kick me out of there. It doesn't make any sense, so they will figure I've been running the count. They're not idiots. So if you're by yourself, you can only change your bets a little bit, or they'll get wise."

"How often does that happen?" I asked. "Are they that sensitive?"

"Hell yeah. They watch that stuff like hawks. I could tell you some stories, believe me," he said, chuckling. "But the point is, if you have a team, you get up from the table when the table gets hot. Then your teammate, who for all the casino knows is a complete stranger, sits down and starts making the big bets. It's much less suspicious that way."

I nodded, beginning to appreciate the scheme. "I guess that makes sense. And you can make a living at this?"

He smiled. "A *good* living. At least, I *could*." His face had gotten somber.

I turned it over in my mind for a few seconds. "Well, I can try to help you. What I'd start with is basic surveillance. The point would be to follow the members and see how they're actually doing. I assume they make reports to you about their winnings and losses?"

"Exactly," he said. "That's the weird thing. It's not just one of them on a losing streak. It's three or four of them. If it were just one of them, then I'd know that one was the thief."

I knew I was going to help Dan, but I was having trouble coming up with *how* I would go about it. Before I could blurt out a question, he anticipated it.

"Before you do any surveillance, though, I had a crazy idea." His eyes were twinkling.

I tried to hide my natural recoil response, but I don't think it worked. As an exotic dancer, I had spent half my life fending off fat men's "crazy ideas." "Okay…?" I said hesitantly.

"Join the team," he said matter-of-factly. "We'll train you up. It's not that hard. You just need to be good with numbers and be able to handle pressure. Then you'll be on the inside."

I laughed out loud. "You want me to be a card counter? I can barely even remember that red means stop and green means go."

"You're too modest, Raven. I read the stories in the paper. That's why I'm here. You're one of the best in the business."

I smiled. In only a few months working as a private investigator, I had lucked into a few high-profile jobs, and the exposure from those had led to a steady stream of new business. At least until the last week, which had been unusually quiet. "What those stories don't report is how much luck has to do with it."

"So we have something in common," he said, chuckling. "Worth a shot, though, no?"

I shrugged. It wasn't like I had anything else to do. "All right. Maybe this will even be fun."

"That's the spirit," he said, beaming. His legs creaked as he stood up, and he winced as he gripped the desk.

"I'm too young for this," he muttered half apologetically.

"My knees crack every time I stand up," I said, trying to sound sympathetic. I pulled out some paperwork and had him sign a retainer agreement, and then I showed him out.

# CHAPTER TWO

———

Dan and I had agreed to meet up again two days later. He'd emailed me with a list of websites to visit as part of a crash course in card counting. As he'd explained, the theory was really quite simple. If you could keep track of how many tens and aces remained in the deck, you could determine whether the deck was favorable or unfavorable to the player. Most of the time, it would be unfavorable. After all, the rules were made by the casinos themselves. But occasionally the deck had a lot of tens in it, which they called a positive count, and those were considered "bust cards" for the dealer. That's when you bet big and tried to beat the house.

It turned out that there were a number of methods to keep track of the card count. In the old days, when casinos used a single deck of cards at each table, it was easy. But most casinos now used six or eight decks, and some of the high-end places even used a card shuffling machine to create a kind of endless deck. Because each deal of the cards came from a "new" deck, it didn't make sense to count cards at those places, so we would have to stick to the more traditional casinos on and off the Strip. But when they used eight decks, the methods for keeping track of so many cards were more complicated than anything I'd ever done.

Dan arrived at my office just before seven on Wednesday night.

"What's that?" I asked, directing my question at the plastic contraption he carried under his arm.

"It's a shoe. I'm sure you've seen one before but never out of context like this."

He placed it on the coffee table in the lobby. The device was about the size of a small shoe box, with a hollow back and an opening on the front. Dan took out a small bag filled with decks of playing cards and began shuffling them on top of the table. Then he arranged them into a neat pile and placed them, facing backwards, into the back of the shoe.

"I'll be the dealer," he said, his face looking mischievous.

I knelt down next to the coffee table and began to concentrate. He dealt out five dummy hands of two cards each, all face up, and then dealt the dealer's hand, which was one up and one down.

I scanned the cards as quickly as possible and added up the total. "Plus two?" I asked hopefully.

He shrugged. "Three. Try again." He whisked up all the cards and then dealt another spread of hands. My mind whirred, trying to keep up.

"It's going to be this fast in the casino," he said not very reassuringly.

"Plus one," I whispered.

"Right! Very good."

We continued this exercise for a solid half hour. Usually, I was right or within one, but I whiffed a few completely. I couldn't tell if he was impressed or frustrated.

"Okay," he said. "Now we'll add real play to the mix. You're going to play your hand *and* keep track of the count. You memorized basic strategy?"

Basic strategy was the well-established method of playing blackjack to get the highest advantage against the house. Most tourists played something close to it with leaks here and there which gave the house an even greater edge.

"I think I've got it," I said. "Except, I sometimes forget when to split and double down."

He smiled knowingly and then gave me a little rhyme to help remember. It was lame, but it was the kind of thing I'd always relied on in school to memorize things.

"Let's go," he said, dealing the cards out of the shoe in a practiced blur. I had gotten a fifteen against the dealer's eight.

"Hit," I muttered.

"Good," he said, dealing out a bust card for me and dummy cards for all the others. I had to remember to keep watch of all their hands to keep the running count. He wound up with a twenty and seemed to take some kind of bizarre pleasure in beating the other invisible players.

An hour flew by. I was making a few mistakes here and there, but on the whole, I was getting into the groove of it.

"So what's the count?" he asked, *again*. We were on at least our twentieth deal using eight decks.

"Minus eleven." It came out a little more confidently than I actually felt.

"*Very* good, Raven." He straightened up in his chair and began rubbing his lower back. "I think you're going to do just fine."

I sighed, mentally exhausted. I couldn't remember the last time my mind had been whirring like that for a full hour. It had required calling on parts of brain matter that had long since been abandoned, but I was enjoying a strange sense of accomplishment.

"Does it get any easier?" I asked.

"You bet it does. Once you get good at it, it's impossible *not* to count the cards, even if you're just playing for fun. Second nature." He was pushing all the cards together on the table and arranging them in the shoe.

I chuckled, recalling an ancient memory. "My plastic surgeon said the same thing. Well, kind of."

Dan stopped arranging the cards and flashed me a puzzled look.

I stood up. "He said once you start rearranging people's body parts, you can never appreciate beauty again. You're always evaluating people. Do they need a smaller nose, bigger boobs, fuller lips, a rounder ass? He said it's exhausting."

I looked down to see Dan giving me the once-over, no doubt trying to guess what kinds of work I'd had done. Dr. Ruiz had given me the best rack money could buy, but apart from that, I was 100% Raven.

"I'm all natural," I said, "except for the…obvious." He was staring at my chest.

Dan stood up, his chubby cheeks flushed with pink. "Of course," he said, coughing nervously. "None of my business."

"So when do I start?" I asked. My phone had been unusually slow all week, so I was eager to get cracking.

"First, we'll try you out in a real casino under battle conditions," he said, happy to change the subject away from plastic surgery.

"Battle conditions?" I asked.

He smiled. "We're a little melodramatic, I admit. But when you're being spied on by a dozen cameras and security guards, it feels a little like battle."

"Got it," I said.

"I've got to get home tonight, or my wife will think I've got a girlfriend. I'm already kind of nervous about that, actually." He coughed again.

"About what?"

"When she sees you, she's going to flip out. Let's just put it that way." He spread his hands apologetically. "I mean, you look like...uh, who's that actress?" He started snapping his fingers impatiently, the name on the tip of his tongue.

"Julia Roberts?" I asked hopefully.

He smiled. "No. Lucy Lawless. That's it."

"Xena, the Warrior Princess?"

"You could be her sister," he said.

"I'll take that as a compliment. But why would your wife ever have to see me?"

He smiled. "She's on the team."

"Ahh."

"In fact, she's kind of the boss." He smiled sheepishly. "Anyway," he said. "Does tomorrow work for you?"

I nodded, and we agreed to meet in the afternoon at Bally's, a big old casino right on the Strip, about a half mile from my condo.

After we parted ways, I closed up the office, headed out into the cool October night, and then drove myself down to Cougar's, a gentlemen's club—and I use the term loosely—where I made most of my money. Opening up a private detective shop was my ticket out of the skin business, and at the moment, I had one high heel out the door. But the money was still too good to walk away entirely, and (I told myself) I needed to build up a stash of money for when I finally cut the cord and became an *ex*-stripper.

Wednesday nights were a hit-or-miss proposition. I definitely still went in to work on Thursdays and the weekend because that's where the most money was. But Wednesdays were weird. Half of Las Vegas revolves around the convention business, and I was no different. Some Wednesdays were duds, while others, like tonight, would no doubt see a flurry of activity from not one but two technology conventions in town for the week. Technology meant men, twenty and thirtysomething men, and not surprisingly, they wanted to experience the full panoply of entertainments Vegas had to offer.

I wasn't disappointed. Arriving just after nine, I had to share a locker with someone named Darcy, a new dancer I'd never met. Darcy had the most amazing fingernails I'd ever seen—iridescent pink with tiny little red hearts inscribed in the middle. She didn't know who *I* was either. Didn't know that seven or eight years ago, my picture had been plastered all around town on thirty-foot billboards and that men lined up to get a five-minute lap dance from me. But that was the nature of the beast. When you rely on looks and nothing else, it's a here-today-gone-tomorrow kind of business, and I was fine with that. Or so I told myself.

None of my regular customers were in the club that night. Or if they were, they weren't seeking me out. But I had managed to catch the eye of an entire table of app developers from Sweden, and I ended up giving private dances for half the table. Apparently, I looked enough like a famous Swedish reality-TV star that the guys opened their wallets more than I would have expected. They proved to be a very well-behaved bunch, all things considered, and I managed to make enough money from them to rationalize quitting early for the night, by which I meant two thirty.

The next day had me meeting up with Dan, my client, at Bally's. On principle, I should have suggested a different location. You see, I'm a member of a fledgling group of eccentric locals called the Apostrophe Society, and it's our mission to get Caesars Entertainment Corporation to add apostrophes to the names of Caesars Palace and Ballys, both of which it owns. To us, the giant illuminated signs on the casinos are an affront, a grammatically incorrect scar on the otherwise beautiful Las Vegas skyline. The truth was, I had only been to one Apostrophe Society meeting, which had proven to be little more than an excuse for a bunch of weirdos to get together and drink. I did enough drinking with weirdos already, so I had steered clear of them since then. But still, I had my principles.

I was waiting near the blackjack tables when a complete stranger tapped me on the shoulder. He had a full build, ruddy beard, dark glasses, and a camouflage John Deere hat.

"Yes?" I asked hesitantly.

He was smiling. "Ready to go?"

I crunched up my face, confused.

"It's me. Dan." He was smiling now.

I chuckled, finally seeing behind the disguise. "I get it now. Nice beard. Is that really necessary?"

"Heck yeah it is," he said. "I'm not even going to play blackjack, either. But I'm banned from every casino on the Strip, so I have to do this nonsense every time I come."

I shrugged. "Seems like a lot of effort."

"Tell me about it. But it pays off." He gestured with his hand. "Let's go find a table."

The two of us made a leisurely circuit around the casino floor. Bally's had two banks of blackjack tables, for a total of twenty-four, but in the middle of the afternoon, only half were in use. Most of them had table minimums of ten dollars, with a couple at twenty-five. Dan was subtly checking out the dealers.

"It's not what you'd think," he murmured. "These young ones are the most gung ho about card counting." He was looking at a twentysomething Asian woman who seemed to have a permanent frown etched on her face. "The old guard, that's what you want. Some guy who's been dealing for twenty years. In the union. Doesn't care too much—just wants to get through his shift."

I nodded, looking around. "How about that guy?" I asked, glancing two tables down the line.

"He's perfect. And the table looks good too. Not too crowded but not empty either," Dan said.

"Why does that matter?" I asked.

"You can't play alone because when you change bets, it'll be obvious. So it's good to have some cover. And when other people increase their bets, you can just pretend you're playing along."

"Okay, I think I'm ready," I lied. My heart was pounding for some reason. *It was only blackjack*, I told myself, *a game I'd played hundreds of times*. I knew how to count and how to play basic strategy, so why was my nervous system acting like I was about to storm Omaha Beach on D-day?

"You got the money?" he asked.

I patted my pocket where ten crisp hundreds were folded neatly.

"Then get in there, soldier! I'll be off by those slots over there, watching." He patted me affectionately on the shoulder and turned away.

# CHAPTER THREE

My throat had gone dry, and my palms were sweaty. I had convinced myself that I couldn't even add one plus two, but somehow I forced myself to sit down at a ten-dollar blackjack table. The dealer's name was Terry. Terry had a paunch that stuck out over the table, an awful 1980s uniform that had been spot cleaned too many times, and a wispy gray mustache. He also had gray eyes, and they were boring into mine.

"Are you going to play or just sit there?" he asked.

In my terror, I had completely frozen, forgetting to place any money on the table.

"Sorry," I said. "Long day." I reached into my pocket and pulled out the hundreds, placing three of them neatly on the table. I hoped no one had noticed my hands shaking.

With practiced ceremony, the dealer took the bills and laid them out next to each other so the cameras overhead could have a clear view and then counted out twelve green chips, each worth twenty-five dollars.

"One stack of red, please," I said softly.

The dealer, nonplussed, pulled back four of the green chips and counted out a much taller stack of reds which were worth only five dollars each. I wasn't quite ready to commit to betting twenty-five bucks every hand, so the reds would give me some flexibility. The other three players at the table, two middle-aged men and an older Korean woman, watched the dealer's hands with practiced indifference. I was sitting in the left-most seat or what Dan had called "third base."

Terry's hairy hands began sliding the cards out of the shoe and onto the table. He flipped each card over and laid it down with an authoritative *thwack* in front of each player. I tried to tune out everything except the numbers. The cards came out seven, four, jack, an ace for me and then the down card for the dealer. And then another seven, queen, three, and a four for me. The dealer was showing a nine. I had ace and 4, a ho-hum hand but one that required a decision since the ace could be treated either as a one or an eleven. Against the dealer's nine, I would treat it as a one. I made that decision in a split second and tried to focus on the others' cards. The woman with two sevens took a hit and busted when she drew a nine. The next guy drew a lucky six to get twenty, but his buddy wasn't so fortunate when a ten busted his thirteen. I was happy to hit and draw a four, giving me nineteen against the dealer's nine—a reasonable chance to push or even win.

We pushed. The dealer showed a king in the hole to give him nineteen as I'd predicted. My eyes scanned all the cards on the table to recheck the count. A number of tens had been played—every face card counts as ten—so the deck was slightly unfavorable now. But since they were already half through with the shoe, I had no idea what had already been played. I wouldn't start counting for real until the next shoe.

The Korean woman seemed to believe it was her God-appointed duty to fill the entire casino with a thick cloud of cigarette smoke. I felt bad for the dealer, who had to keep turning away to cough and who wasn't shy about brushing away any plumes of smoke that strayed into his face. She puffed on, undeterred or oblivious. Over the next several hands, my heart rate started to drop, and I began to ease into a semblance of rhythm, playing my own hand and keeping track of all the other cards. The dealer wasn't one of the lightning-fast ones I'd seen, but he wasn't slow, either. Lucky for me, his constant need to cough or brush away smoke gave me a few seconds to catch up when I got behind.

I sat and played for about a half hour, which was probably four full shoes. The first one was unlucky, starting out with a bevy of aces and tens, and the second and third were about average. Up a little, down a little, with no pattern at all. I varied my bets slightly, just to mix things up, but I was treading water, down about eighty bucks. The fourth shoe, though, was when my heart started pounding again. Right from the get-go, it was all little cards. As the sixes, threes, and fours splayed out on the table over and over again, I slowly increased my bets. From twenty-five to thirty-five. And then to fifty. And when I started winning, up to a hundred. And then, just as I was gathering steam, a new dealer came in and tapped Terry on the shoulder.

Dan had trained me to be paranoid (not that I needed much help), and the new dealer got my stomach heaving and churning. I was certain that someone upstairs had noticed me changing my bets to take advantage of the count, and the new dealer, a scary-looking guy named Viktor, was probably an expert on busting card counters and calling in security.

But Viktor looked as bored as Terry had, as though our cards were the least interesting things he'd ever seen. I looked around and saw other dealers being relieved, and I realized Viktor was merely Terry's regular relief dealer. Dealers got breaks every forty minutes, and Terry was no different. Back to business. I had temporarily lost track of the exact count, but I knew there had been no shift in the massively pro-player tendency of the deck. Hundred-dollar bets were my new norm, and then $125, and even $150. Double down? You betcha. Split aces? Done. No one batted an eyelash. With adrenaline coursing through me, I raked in piles of black chips, trying to conceal them in little, nondescript mounds.

But Viktor noticed, as he was trained to do. "Let me give you purple for that," he said in a thick Eastern European or Russian accent following one of my wins and exchanged a purple $500 chip for a few of my blacks. He still seemed bored.

"Thanks," I whispered, my throat completely dry.

A couple more wins got me some more purple, and then an insane hand where I split three aces and drew three tens gave me 21, 21, 21 and six hundred bucks. And then the shoe was done. I couldn't believe it was over. My hands were shaking again, but now it was from pure thrill rather than nervousness.

"You can color me up," I said, standing up and pushing my chips into the center of the felt.

"Nice work," Viktor muttered, flashing me a phony smile. Now that it was time for his tip, he'd suddenly become very friendly.

Everyone at the table was mesmerized by the chips being stacked in little piles and moved around. Greens and reds became black, and blacks became purples, and purples turned into $1000 yellow chips. I made sure to keep my head down, certain that the cameras would take note of so much money going out of a ten-dollar table, but I couldn't take my eyes off the chips. Finally, Viktor pushed a small stack over to me consisting of two yellow chips, one purple, and seven black, green, and reds. Viktor had only been at the table for five minutes, but I knew it was customary to be generous, so I flipped him a black one as I left.

I turned and began walking away at random, my brain running on overdrive. Dan caught up with me as I neared the hotel lobby where a half-naked cabaret dancer with a two-foot feathery hat stood greeting new guests.

"Check this out," I said, opening up my hands to reveal my loot.

Dan was taken aback. "Twenty-nine hundred? In a half hour? You're *good. Too* good."

"Huh?"

"I was watching. You upped your bets a little aggressively. Someday, they're going to notice that kind of action and back you right off. And then you'll be done."

I nodded. I was still enjoying the afterglow of winning almost three grand for doing nothing, so I wasn't going to let him bring me down.

"What was the count at that point?" he asked.

"Plus eleven, I think," I said.

Dan whistled. "That's a real heater of a shoe. That kind of thing is pretty rare. Maybe one in fifty, something like that. But you see how profitable that *could* have been?"

I frowned. "What do you mean? It was *very* profitable!" I showed him the yellow chips again to make the point.

He smiled. "I know. I know. But imagine if you had a partner. A guy with ten grand in his pocket. When the table gets red hot like that, you give him a secret signal, and he sits down and plunks down two thousand a hand."

I nodded enthusiastically. The light bulb had finally gone off in my head. "You could make fifty grand in ten minutes," I said.

Dan smiled. "Now you're getting it."

"So what's next?" I asked, fingering the chips in my hand.

"Well, we've got a meeting tomorrow night. I think you're ready for me to introduce you to the others, don't you?"

I smiled. "I'm ready. I was a little nervous at first there, but with each shoe, it became easier and easier to keep track."

"Exactly," he said. "Like I said, it almost becomes second nature. Now let's get out of here. My beard is itchy."

Dan told me where to meet the next night, and I headed to the cashier's cage to turn my colored plastic chips into green paper. The cashier, a middle-aged woman with a wide face and a distracted air, wasn't particularly impressed with my haul, but I didn't mind. The sound of all those bills shuffling between her perfectly manicured fingers was on par with any symphony.

In my job as a stripper, dealing with wads of cash was commonplace, but I'm quite sure I had never palmed a wad that had twenty-nine hundred-dollar bills in it. There was a heft to it, a *presence*, and it was exerting a powerful force over me. I couldn't keep my right hand from fondling the money even after it was lodged deep in my pocket. *My precious.* There was something about the whole thing that felt *right* to me, an excitement I attributed to the fact that I had just pocketed a boatload of cash by using my brain instead of my boobs. Even though card counting wasn't any more socially acceptable than stripping, I didn't care. It was a start.

My brain had an annoying habit of making lemonade into lemons. True to form, my glee at winning began shifting into a vague nervousness, a creeping paranoia that everyone around me—and even the unseen security guys operating the "eye in the sky" cameras—knew not only that I was holding lots of cash but that I had won it by counting cards. I knew it was crazy, but I just wanted to get out of there, and fast. Feeling like I'd just robbed a bank, I skedaddled out through the main hotel lobby and onto the Strip, making sure to keep my head down so the cameras couldn't get too good a look at me, although they had already seen plenty of me at the cage where they had more cameras than an Academy Awards red carpet.

I lollygagged at home for most of the evening, succumbing to the familiar lure of my patented triple grilled cheese sandwich into which I snuck some tuna casserole, a tomato, and possibly four slices of salami. And then at nine, I dragged myself over to Cougar's to work the Thursday night shift.

Cougar's slayed any lingering buzz I was feeling after winning so much money at blackjack. It was the damned locker room scales. One of the few fringe benefits of working as a stripper is that you get paid to burn calories. One of the girls had calculated long ago that an average night meant a thousand calories—four or five hours of pole dancing and wriggling around on guys' laps would make those calories melt away, so you could eat just about anything and not gain weight. As my detective business had grown in recent months, I had cut back *slightly* on my night job. Instead of five nights a week, I was down to four and sometimes three if it was a slow week. Whoever coined the phrase "no good deed goes unpunished" was a genius. Having taken real steps to transform my life for the better, my reward was to get fatter. And *fast*. The locker room scale treated me as though I had been on a month-long cruise with a suite right next to the twenty-four-hour pasta bar. When no one was looking, I tried standing on the scale on the other side of the locker room, with even *worse* results. How was it possible to gain four pounds in three weeks just by skipping a measly three or four nights at the club?

I tried to mask my perma-scowl all night without much success. Instead of my normal twelve or fifteen lap dances—which is where we make our real money—I was only asked to dance for a half-dozen guys, and only one of whom gave me a tip worth mentioning. Was it my mood, I wondered, or had they noticed the extra four pounds?

These were the pleasant thoughts that kept repeating themselves in my mind as I tried in vain to get to sleep at a reasonable hour. A marathon of *House Hunters* on HGTV finally did the trick somewhere between an annoying couple shopping for a mansion in Belize and an impossibly cute lesbian couple shopping for a Parisian *pied-à-terre*.

# CHAPTER FOUR

———

In the morning, my own bathroom scale betrayed me even worse than the ones at Cougar's had. Hoping to be greeted warmly by a trusted ally, I had instead been stabbed in the chest with a dull blade by a traitor lurking in my very own home. Reasoning that a mini vacation would allow the scale to take stock and reconsider, I removed the battery for a few seconds and then replaced it, allowing it a complete reboot or lobotomy. But instead of appreciating the time off, the vile little machine claimed I had gained two-tenths of a pound! In less than a minute! *Screw it*, I thought. I flipped the scale over and switched it to metric. That would show it who was in charge.

I made breakfast but didn't enjoy it, my brain still fixated on my weight gain. Even though I knew eggs were healthy, every bite had me feeling like the nine-hundred-pound swine at the state fair. And, as if I needed another buzzkill, I knew a long session in the gym lurked in my imminent future.

As it turned out, the gym was just what I needed. For one thing, I was by far the thinnest, sexiest person in the whole place. I *loved* working out alone! But really, sweating away on the treadmill got me thinking philosophically about what was really important, and I realized that in the grand scheme of things, four pounds wasn't very important. After all, it was less than two kilograms! Even so, I resolved to get past my lingering denial of my new reality—I had to eat better and exercise more. So, instead of jumping off the treadmill after forty minutes, I stayed on and powered through another set of commercials, most of which were pitching things like reverse mortgages, prescription drugs, and bankruptcy lawyers—the trifecta of daytime TV ads. And when I was all done, I had burned a whopping 412 calories. *Which made me very, very hungry.* And lunch wasn't even a blip on the radar screen yet. "No good deed goes unpunished," I grumbled to myself.

The rest of the day I resolved to stop thinking about food and weight, which only made me think about food even more. So I whipped out a couple dusty decks of cards and forced myself to practice keeping the running count. I would deal through both decks, scanning each card and registering whether it added or subtracted from the count, knowing that the count at the end of both decks had to be zero. Once I got through them a few times, I increased the speed, forcing my brain out of its comfort zone as the numbers whizzed by. And it wasn't just numbers. The brain had to recognize that a colorfully designed picture with a $Q$ or $J$ on it counted as a ten. It was becoming easier, but it wasn't second nature just yet. Not with *this* brain.

I was scheduled to meet up with Dan and his team at six. I had grown used to having nothing to do on Friday nights, but it was nice to have a date, of sorts, even if it involved meeting a bunch of geeky card counters. And there had been a vague promise regarding pizza. But the meeting was at a church. That's the weird part of it. Located between downtown Vegas and the Strip, it was called The Meadows Worship Center, a reference to the English meaning of "Las Vegas." The church itself was an old gray industrial building made out of concrete blocks, but it greeted visitors with a gaudy, colorful sign that said *Welcome* in a half-dozen languages. Surrounding it was a series of smaller buildings, including one marked *Annex B* which is where our meeting was to be held. The neighborhood itself was kind of sketchy, but I figured that's what allowed them to afford such a big complex.

I admit to having a few butterflies in my stomach as I parked my car, a brand new Porsche Cayenne convertible, which I had bought partly with the insurance money I received after my Audi had been smashed to smithereens a few weeks earlier. The butterflies weren't because I was nervous about the car being stolen. Instead, I was apprehensive about walking into a room full of strangers, strangers who would be judging my card-counting skills and thus my overall worthiness to be in their presence.

In light of Dan's concerns about his wife, who he obviously feared, I had worn my loosest-fitting jeans and a Burberry Oxford shirt I had bought on a drunken whim and that I'd never even taken the tags off of. It was classy, in a distinctly middle-class sort of way. "Hey, look at me," it screamed. "I'm an expensive name brand!" But the point was no cleavage, no curves, all business.

A half-dozen people were milling about in the room, which looked like a repurposed machine shop. White painted walls, high ceilings, and no ornamentation, but the wood floors had been refinished so that they gleamed with a welcoming, comforting glow under the shop lights. Dan spotted me and gave me a subtle once-over. "Thank you," he mouthed, referring to my deliberately buttoned-down appearance.

He came over and shepherded me around to meet the others. The first was a six-three stick of a man-boy with frizzy red hair falling over his forehead and fashionable glasses.

Dan introduced him. "This is O'Scannlain, but we just call him O. Don't worry. He cleans up *very* well. He's been with us about six months, right?"

O nodded, his head bobbing up and down like some kind of giant owl. "Before that, I worked behind a desk, night shift, doing telemarketing. This is *much* better."

"I can imagine!" I said, craning my neck upwards.

Dan took me around to the others. Among them were a dark-skinned, middle-aged man named Dinesh who had an earnest face and smooth black hair and a young woman named Neva who I placed as Russian or Ukrainian. She seemed not to like me right from the outset. There was also a blond guy from California who looked like he'd just washed up on the beach and a short squat man with an egg-shaped head who was garbed head to toe in Chicago sports team attire. He told me just to call him Jordan, after his favorite basketball player.

We milled around for another few minutes with additional team members trickling in. The last to join us was Dan's wife. When she entered, everyone in the room grew still, like a swarm of noisy crickets that suddenly sensed danger. Her physical presence was anything but intimidating. She stood five foot four, maybe, with short brown hair and a round face, her clothes even more conservative than mine. She was pretty enough, in her own way, and I couldn't resist doing a mental makeover on her. Grow out the hair, add some color to the face, and by God, get rid of those clothes. And *smile*, woman! She was standing in the doorway regarding us with obvious displeasure, but when her gaze finally fell upon me, her face brightened, and she approached.

"Laura Hartman," she said, extending a hand. She was looking me over without being obvious about it. "You'll do," she said simply. "With the right tweaks, you'll blend in anywhere." And then she focused on my face. "You have a good complexion for this. Almost olive. You could be Jersey-Italian one day, Spanish the next. Um, maybe Puerto Rican? It's a stretch, but it might work."

Dan came over to consult. With the two of them inspecting me, I felt like a carcass at a meat auction. Obviously, they were considering what kind of disguises I could use, should the need arise. "You speak Spanish?" Dan asked.

"No," I said.

Dan chuckled. "'No' is how you say 'no' in Spanish, so you do speak *some* Spanish. Technically."

Laura and I rolled our eyes in unison. "I have to live with him," she muttered, seeking sympathy. Then she turned abruptly and clapped her hands loudly. "Let's begin."

The ten of us found seats at two long tables which were pushed into a kind of *V*. Dan began by reintroducing me, and once again, I felt all the eyes examining my face. Were the others trying to imagine me in various disguises, too?

After a little small talk, the meeting soon grew boring, a problem compounded by the fact that I was getting very hungry. Laura began working on a laptop computer and showing PowerPoint slides of the team's performance over the last month. The faces in the room were stony and grim as she went through the numbers. Some of it was hard to follow, but most of it made sense to me. One of the most important metrics was the baseline expectation—the amount they'd expect to lose per hour just playing "normal" blackjack where the house had about a one-percent edge even if the player played perfectly. Then, for my benefit, Laura explained what their expectations were when the odds shifted to the players' advantage. At a plus-one-percent table, which was quite common, the player was expected to raise his bets slightly. At a plus-two table, a little bit more. At these kinds of tables, there was an expected profit, although it was nothing to write home about. But at plus-three percent or higher, when there were *lots* of tens still in the deck, the player would issue the secret signal to alert his partner to join the table and start betting really big. *That* was where the real money was made, as Dan had already explained to me.

"The problem," Laura explained, "is that we don't seem to be hitting anything big when the table is really strongly in our favor. When you're betting big and losing, that wipes out all the smaller gains."

There was some gentle murmuring, but she pretended not to hear.

"The long and short of it is, guys…" she said then paused, possibly to soften the blow, "we need some additional OOP."

More murmuring. Before I could ask what OOP meant, Dan touched my arm and leaned over. "Out of pocket," he whispered.

Laura continued. "It doesn't have to be much, but we're thinking three thousand each to seed a new run."

The guy on my right sighed audibly. Looking around, I could tell no one was happy about this turn of events, but their expressions were resigned, most of them probably expecting it. They were going to have to dig into their own pockets to keep the venture going.

"It doesn't have to be today," Laura said. "But by next week Friday. And then we can go out there and start winning again like in the old days. For now, we only have a kitty of eighteen thousand and change which will have to last us."

The others were glancing at each other uncomfortably. I sensed a bit of rebellion in the room, an unwillingness to roll over, but the numbers were the numbers. If they wanted to continue, they needed to fund themselves, and they were all intelligent enough to understand that.

"So," the California surfer guy began, "are we working this weekend? Eighteen thousand is enough to stake a couple teams."

Laura nodded. "Yes. We want to break Raven in, so we wouldn't want a full stake anyway," she said. "No offense," she whispered, looking at me.

I smiled, remaining silent.

"We haven't been to Canyon Creek in a while," the surfer guy said, his voice serious and refined, nothing like what I expected. "And last time we were there, we did okay, right? Maybe this will break the streak."

Dan was nodding along next to me. "Good idea," he said. He looked to his wife for approval, and she offered a curt nod.

Dan stood up. "Raven's going to be joining Team 2, so let's have them go to Canyon Creek. Raven, that means you're paired with Dinesh, Tyler, and O'Scannlain." He pointed at the three guys who were sitting together at the other table. "They'll fill you in."

There was a knock at the door, and Laura went to answer it. The faces of the others in the room brightened noticeably.

"Pizza," Dan whispered, joining his wife at the door.

Dan and Laura schlepped in eight boxes of pizza from Mamma Mia's, a place I'd heard of but never tried.

"*Eight* pizzas?" I asked to no one in particular. It was kind of like visiting my family. Ten people, food for thirty.

Tyler, my new card-counting partner, smiled knowingly, revealing two rows of gleaming teeth. "There will be leftovers," he said excitedly. "*Lots* of leftovers."

"Well, I'm impressed," I said, meaning it. The smell in the room was intoxicating.

"I'm Tyler, by the way," he said somewhat shyly. He was a cutie pie, this Tyler, with curly blond locks falling partly over his inky-blue eyes. He had a teenager's haircut and mannerisms, but on further inspection, he was probably in his late twenties.

"Raven," I said, offering a hand, which he shook tentatively.

"We've got some work to do here," Tyler said, eyeing the mountain of pizza. I helped him open up the boxes and spread them out on both tables. Tyler went straight for a deluxe pizza that seemed to have at least ten toppings on it. But I was happy to see my old standby, a simple pie with just pepperoni and black olives on it. That was the standard by which I usually judged a pizza joint, so I figured I'd start there.

I grabbed a few slices and sat down next to Tyler. The amazing smell of cured meat and tomato sauce had my stomach going on overdrive, so I dug in, oblivious to everything else. When I looked up, having devoured my first piece, I noticed that I was the only one eating. The others had sat down and seemed to be awkwardly waiting in silence. I made eye contact with Dan who offered me a thin smile and held up a single finger which I took as a sign to take a break from gorging myself.

"Dear Father," Dan began, spreading his arms apart. "We thank you for this bounty and for providing us with the means to provide for ourselves and our families by fighting to punish sin in all its forms, and we humbly ask your blessing on this meal, just as we ask your good fortune for our work in the days and weeks and months to come. Amen."

"Amen," echoed the room.

During the prayer, my face had grown as red as the pepperoni. I was used to looking like an idiot, but this was one for the idiot record books, a faux pas made worse by the fact that I was just meeting this crowd for the first time. Why hadn't Dan clued me in? How hard would it have been to say, "Hey, Miss Piggy, I know you can't wait to stuff your pie hole, but we're going to say a little prayer first." But then I realized I couldn't blame Dan. After all, we were meeting in a *church*. Was it really so surprising that they'd pray before digging into their pizza? That realization only made me more embarrassed.

Tyler elbowed me. "Don't sweat it," he whispered. "No biggie. Here, try some of mine." He held out a wedge of the deluxe, which I felt compelled to try.

"Wow, that's really pretty good," I said, genuinely impressed. I had been so hungry that I hadn't even noticed how my first slice tasted, but the deluxe seemed like it was even better. It was salty, owing to all the cured meats and green olives crammed onto the thin crust.

Tyler and I made chitchat for a few minutes, but mostly we were focused on filling our stomachs with copious quantities of food. I had to force myself to be mindful of appearances and to slow down, especially after blowing the pre-meal prayer. I leaned over in Tyler's direction. "What did Dan mean in the prayer when he said something about providing for ourselves by punishing sin?"

Tyler smiled and finished chewing. "That's the funny part. Or ironic, I guess. We all believe gambling to be sinful activity. It wrecks people, destroys relationships, you name it. And so part of our mission is to punish the casinos themselves by hitting them where it hurts the most."

I nodded. "Got it," I said. "Hopefully, the luck will change for the better."

"You're telling me," he said, half sighing. "This is a wicked stretch we're on. I've been doing okay, but I guess the others aren't getting the hits when they need them."

"Is that pretty common?" I asked. I was growing a liking for Tyler, so I felt a little bad about spying on him. But not *too* bad.

He shrugged. "It happens sometimes. You have to remember that even at an awesome table, you can lose your shirt. The player could have a ten-point edge, but that's all it is—an edge. We're going to win six times out of ten, and in the long term, we make money. But the house can get very lucky sometimes. It can go on winning streaks too. And if you have five grand out there, a single hand can ruin your whole week."

"And that's what's been happening?" I probed.

"Basically," Tyler said. "You wait hours to get a great table, bring in your partner, and then the dealer somehow manages to win. So not only do you not win, but you lose a small fortune. That's what's been happening, I guess."

"You guess?"

"Well, I mean, not to *me*. Our team has been running okay. Not great, but okay. Up maybe ten grand in the last month. But I guess the others are having some problems."

I nodded. I didn't want to press too much since it felt like pouring salt in the wound. And apparently, we'd be spending some time together over the weekend, so there was no need to keep pumping him for information.

The conversation in the room began picking up as people finished eating. As predicted, there were still about four pizzas left over.

I couldn't resist asking. "So why so many pizzas? Do you do this every week?"

Tyler pushed his plate away and smiled. "It's deductible. See, this is a business meeting. We all get leftovers to have for breakfast or whatever, and the whole thing is a write-off for the business."

I chuckled. "You guys have it all worked out, don't you?"

He shrugged. "We aren't real big on the federal government either, so we try to avoid paying taxes as much as possible, too. It's all on the up and up, of course. You should see what the big corporations get to deduct. This is *nothing*."

I leaned back, stuffed, and began trying to process everything. It was an interesting bunch. Tyler was nice, cute, and ringless—the dating trifecta—and yet there was a streak about him I couldn't quite get a grasp on. Idealism, that was it. Whether I agreed with him or not, it was clear he actually believed in things, had principles, and tried to live up to them. That was rare, at least in most of the men I came in contact with.

A gentle touch on my shoulder caused me to turn around.

"I'm Dinesh," the man said with a kindly smile.

I stood up and shook his hand, which was delicate and clammy.

"We are going to kick some butt tomorrow. I can feel it!" His enthusiasm was contagious.

Tyler chuckled. "Dinesh is our resident optimist. He's also the big better. Usually, he plays the part of a rich foreigner. Who are you going to be tomorrow, Dinesh? Prince Akbar? Mr. Salaam? Who's that guy who doesn't talk, only uses hand gestures?"

Dinesh grinned broadly, his eyes sparkling. "Dr. Gupta," he said. Clearly, Dinesh enjoyed the game of playing the casinos for fools. "We will wait and see, Mr. Tyler," he said, using a deliberately thick singsongy Indian accent.

The man known as O joined us. He wasn't as smiley as the rest, didn't share in their unbridled optimism. "Three grand, man. Where am I gonna get three grand?"

Dinesh pooh-poohed him. "We'll spot you, O. Just like last time."

O grimaced, the memory a painful one. "Yeah, yeah, I know. Maybe tomorrow's the day. You have good luck, Raven?"

I shrugged. "I'm part Irish, if that helps."

He snorted. "I'm one hundred percent, baby, and look where it got me. I'm forty-one, flat broke, and counting cards for a living."

Tyler chimed in. "But you are in a community," he said. "Don't forget about your friends, and Jesus."

O nodded, serious now. "You're right, of course." He turned to me. "Before this, my life was even worse, so I guess I shouldn't complain."

Dinesh was still all smiles, bursting with energy. "This is so exciting," he bubbled. "A new member. I can feel it," he bubbled. "This is our time!"

"Down boy," O said, clapping Dinesh on the back. He turned to me. "Raven, we usually work based on when the shift change is. We want to hit them for a few hours and then get a whole new set of fresh dealers to hit. Make sense?"

I nodded. "Yeah. Probably makes it less likely that anyone would notice what you're up to."

"Exactly. So the shift change at Canyon Creek is at eight p.m. Want to start at six?"

"Sounds good," I said.

"Just remember," O said. "You don't know us, and we don't know you. You just play your game, change up your bets a little bit, and use the signal if the table gets hot. Dinesh will know what to do."

"Got it."

# CHAPTER FIVE

———

Saturday had me pacing around my condo, a ball of nervous energy. It brought me back to my first night as a stripper, which felt like a lifetime ago. I had done it almost on a dare, talked into it by my college roommate, and when the day finally arrived, I couldn't keep anything in my stomach. All I remember about my first lap dance was that I got a five-dollar tip and that I was so hungry I almost fainted right on top of the customer.

I wasn't sure how to explain the butterflies this time. It was just cards, after all, and I'd already shown I could keep up during my session at Bally's. But now that I was part of a team, the others were depending on me not to choke and botch the count. And then there was the cloak-and-dagger aspect to it as well. Our team was trying to pull a fast one on the casino, but what the other guys didn't know was that I was trying to put one over on them, too. I was on their team, and I hoped we'd win, but my mission was much different than theirs. In short, I was a spy. It was a lot of lies to keep straight.

Since I was finding it impossible to relax at home, I decided to head over to the casino early to have some dinner there. I figured that if I could get comfortable with the layout of the place, it would calm my nerves enough to allow my brain to function.

It was a decent enough theory, but it didn't work. Given my nervous stomach, it probably wasn't a good idea to have ordered the extra spicy wings, which were a last-minute impulse brought on by the fact that the guy next to me at the bar had ordered some, and they looked fantastic. Plus, they were half price! It wasn't like I had a choice.

I managed to distract myself by playing the slot machine built into the bar, which was a twenty-five center with a number of games, all of which offered terrible odds. People liked the idea of getting "free" drinks at the bar, but the math never quite worked out in the player's favor. But for me, it must have been my lucky night because I hit two small jackpots in the space of twenty minutes. By six, I was up a hundred and nine bucks, and more importantly, my nerves had improved to the point where I felt at least halfway comfortable about what I was about to do.

On the casino floor, there was no sign of Dinesh, Tyler, or O'Scannlain. But that wasn't surprising. Being card-counting veterans on multiple watch lists, they'd be wearing some kind of outfit designed to draw attention away from their facial features. Since I was a newbie, I didn't need to play that game, at least not yet.

The Canyon Creek Resort was five miles off-Strip and appealed to tourists and locals alike—ample parking, decent slot odds, and none of the crowds of nineteen-year-olds who plagued most of the Strip properties. On the casino floor, I found a pre-dinner crowd with some boisterous local types enjoying the fact that it was the weekend. An unusually large contingent of Wisconsin Badgers football fans was milling around, taking in the game on the TVs that were perched above each blackjack table.

The buoyant, festive atmosphere gave me some hope as I did a walk around. With all the buzz on the floor, I figured a dealer would have less reason to focus on me and the way I was betting. Based on Dan's advice, I zeroed in on a sixty-something woman with too much makeup who was dealing to a half empty ten-dollar table. I smiled, plunked down three hundred bucks, and slid myself onto a stool, a young Hispanic couple on my right and a geeky middle-aged guy on my left. No one at the table was smoking.

I played out the rest of the shoe, trying to get myself relaxed before I began counting. I should have just waited it out. A string of six losses in a row had me doubting my prospects for the night, but I was only betting ten bucks a hand, so the bad streak didn't put me too far in the hole. The dealer's strong run apparently wiped out the guy on my left, who sighed audibly and muttered something as he stood up and left. Now it was just me and the couple on my right. They had a small mountain of chips in front of them, a promising sign, and were slurping away at some kind of clear beverage on the rocks. They had been tipping the dealer generously, even when she was killing us, so I sensed they were in for the long haul.

The next shoe wasn't much better. Ups, downs, but no consistent pattern in the card count. I varied my bets anyway, as Dan had suggested, so that when the count was good, it wouldn't seem strange if I upped my bets. Thirty minutes in and my three hundred was almost wiped out. I was down to forty bucks' worth of chips, which felt like scared money, so I plunked down another two Benjamins on the table and got a pile of red and green chips. Reinforcements.

An hour in and still nothing. The couple on my right were killing the dealer despite their obvious ignorance of blackjack strategy. They were playing on feel, pretty much the same way most people played. *That must be fun*, I thought, jealous. I knew that Dan was right, that once I had begun counting cards, I would never be able to "play" blackjack just for fun. It had become work, and it wasn't as interesting as I thought it would be.

Still plodding along, I began giving up on my own prospects and staked my hopes on my partners, who must have been having more success than I was. But things changed for the better during the dealer's twenty-minute break. A fill-in named Bennie, a smiley phone booth-shaped Filipino, seemed to enjoy parceling out the casino's money to the table. We couldn't lose. The count got higher and higher, and so did my heart rate. After an unlikely spread of little cards was played, the count was good enough that I awkwardly made the prearranged signal behind my back—a clenched fist which I held for three or four seconds, and then I took a long swig of my Diet Coke. I just didn't know if Dinesh was watching.

He was. With surprising speed, a thin dark-skinned man in a purple tracksuit appeared and sat down on my left. It was clearly Dinesh, but he had parted his hair differently and was sporting a thin moustache, which might or might not have been real. With practiced nonchalance, he lit up a cigarette and placed a five-hundred-dollar chip in the betting circle. The dealer did a double take but remained silent and smiley as he pulled the cards out of the shoe and placed them in front of us. Even at off-Strip properties, dealers in Vegas were accustomed to big bets from the most unlikely of sources. Giant bets could come from guys dressed like tycoons, but more often, they came from guys in track suits or T-shirts. Dinesh's getup was spot-on.

The dealer dished out ace, ten, ten, and a seven for Dinesh. Bad news. The dealer had a ten showing, which meant Dinesh had a good chance of losing by drawing a ten to get seventeen. But then he got lucky—very lucky—and caught one of the few small cards remaining in the deck, a three. He took a hit and drew another ten, giving him twenty. *Nice.*

I figured Dinesh would push with the dealer, but the dealer ended up with only eighteen, so Dinesh won outright. He pressed his bet and won again, now up fifteen hundred. I was so nervous that I had almost lost track of the count, more focused on Dinesh's play than my own measly fifty-dollar hands. Dinesh added to his bet, making it fifteen hundred dollars on the felt. And then the cards began spewing out exactly in the way we hoped. The couple next to me drew twenties, I had an eighteen, and Dinesh had hit a 21, giving him a $2250 profit from the single hand. He smiled, raking in the chips. But then, as the dealer was completing his own hand, he drew out the yellow plastic card which signaled the end of the shoe.

Dinesh's eyes had gotten big, and not in a good way. The shoe was done, and so was he. He flipped a green chip to the dealer as a tip and politely declined the dealer's offer to "color him up" by exchanging all Dinesh's smaller chips for larger denominations. Dinesh had made almost four grand in just a few minutes, but he hadn't seemed happy.

A lingering sense of unease crept into my consciousness, the cards passing in front of me in a blur. The next three shoes were uneventful, but I managed to make about five hundred bucks in a short little run around nine o'clock. By the time I got up to leave, I figured I was up about nine hundred. I'd started out slow and then down, but during the short burst when Dinesh was at our table, I'd made it all back and then some.

By prearranged rule, our group was not to meet up on casino property, where cameras were everywhere. Instead, we met up at a Burger King a half mile up the highway. I was the last one there.

The expressions on the others' faces confirmed my vague sense that I had screwed something up.

"Hi, Raven." Dinesh, sans moustache, flashed a forced smile.

"Okay, I think I get it," I said, trying to preempt their criticism.

O'Scannlain was unwrapping what looked like a Double Whopper. "Get what?"

I couldn't take my eyes off the Whopper. "The shoe was almost done when I gave the signal. Right?"

Tyler smiled at me, seeming relieved. "You did fine, Raven. I lost a little, but Dinesh made about four grand. But yeah, the timing was a little off there."

Dinesh was dipping about a half-dozen fries into a pool of ketchup. "The thing is, we only get one chance. Maybe two. I guarantee you that right now security is reviewing the tapes of the weirdo in the track suit who made off with four thousand bucks in about five minutes."

I nodded. They had a point. "So if you're going to hit them, hit them big. If I had called you in sooner, you might have hit them for twenty grand. Is that it?"

The three of them were looking at each other. Tyler spoke up. "Rookie mistake. Don't worry about it. He reached into his pocket and pulled a ten-dollar bill from a thick envelope. Go grab some food, Raven. You're skin and bones!"

I chuckled, appreciative of the compliment. It was hard to resist the smell of hot fries and grilled beef, but I was on my way to the club later and didn't want to be gyrating around with a stomach full of fast food.

"Thanks," I said, "but I kind of *want* to look like I'm just skin and bones. Unfortunately, that seems to be what men are looking for. No Whoppers for me."

Tyler shrugged. "It's your loss. It comes out of the winnings. At least eat *something*, eh?" He slid the ten-dollar bill across the table at me.

"Fine," I said, taking it.

I was surprised to find a grilled chicken salad on the menu, and apparently, it also came as a surprise to the cashier, who didn't know which button to push. With help from a manager, she finally figured it out.

"It figures," O'Scannlain said when I returned. He was eyeing my plastic box of salad skeptically. "We get a dame on board, and she goes straight for the greens and sprouts."

"I'm guessing you're a single man. Is that right?" I asked him, giving him my best phony smile.

The other two chuckled.

O'Scannlain leaned back in his seat and rubbed his belly. "I had a girl once," he said wistfully. "But she didn't appreciate me."

"Um hmm," I muttered, digging into my salad. "Her loss," I muttered, chewing my food.

We traded barbs for another five minutes, with Tyler and Dinesh enjoying the show, usually taking my side.

"Don't forget to have her sign," Dinesh said.

Tyler nodded and pulled out the thick envelope. "Count it then sign on the back."

"But be a little discreet," Dinesh whispered. "We don't want to look like drug dealers!"

I chuckled and began thumbing through the money. Four thousand two hundred five dollars, exactly the amount written on the back. The other three had signed underneath that figure.

"Plus mine," I said.

Dinesh nodded. "Right. You count yours out, and then one of us will sign again."

I carefully counted out the $795 I'd cashed in. It was a little less than I'd figured, probably due to the brain's natural tendency to exaggerate the good and minimize the bad. I placed it in the manila envelope, added the total to the others' winnings, and signed next to it. Then Dinesh licked it, sealed it, and signed across the seal.

"This is how they like us to do it," he said, almost apologetically. "We all trust each other, and we're good Christians. But by being anal about it, it means we don't ever have to worry about anything."

I nodded. "Makes sense to me," I lied. They were ignoring the obvious fact that I could have stashed away half my winnings before I handed it over. I supposed the idea was that we all trusted each other, and by signing the envelope, we were vouching for each other. It made it impossible for whoever turned in the money to take a little off the top after we turned our winnings over, which was something, at least. We parted on good terms and agreed we'd go over the details of our winning run at the next full-group meeting where all of our moves would be analyzed by everyone else.

I had packed an outfit for Cougar's, so I was able to go straight to the club and get there by ten when it would just be hitting its busiest rush. I wound up being about ten minutes late, though—the line at the McDonald's drive-thru was *brutal*.

# CHAPTER SIX

—————

I spent the weekend doing my normal routine. Out of bed by eleven, putter around the apartment, work out, shop, obsess about where my life had gone wrong, eat too much. Saturday night I decided to dance an extra hour at the club, hoping to burn away a few extra calories, but instead, I spent most of the time walking around begging drunk guys to buy lap dances. I used to look at other girls doing the same thing and think how pathetic they were, and I wondered if any of the younger girls were thinking the same thing about me. Was it that I was getting older? Or just fatter? Did they notice the extra weight, or was it just an unlucky night? *I need to stop doing this*, I kept telling myself.

Sunday meant church at St. Christopher's, a place that never shied away from taking up *two* collections during the same service. I never minded contributing to the parish expenses—the air conditioning bill alone must have been a million a year, and I was *not* about to sit there and roast like a ham hock—but the second collection offended my skinflint sensibilities. The collection that morning sounded legit (something about medical treatment for poor people in Ecuador), so I threw a ten in the bowl and prayed that it might make up for a few of my sins. Whom was I kidding? Given my history, washing away my sins was going to take a hell of a lot more than ten bucks.

With no plans the rest of Sunday, I called up my friend Cody and convinced him that a hike at Red Rock Canyon would be a good idea. The ninety-seven-degree afternoon had other ideas, though, and after only a half hour, we both looked like we'd been swimming in Lake Mead—when it still had water. Even dripping with sweat, Cody still managed to look beautiful, like the guy on the cover of a steamy romance novel, only less cheesy. Damn him. Five years earlier, he had been the star of a male revue show, and now he was living the life of a wealthy divorcee, thanks to the fact that I had proved his wife was a murderer.

We were standing on an outcropping four-hundred feet in the air, admiring the expansive view of desert, wildlife, and shimmering colorful rock formations. I wasn't usually a mushy romantic when it came to that kind of thing, but the rocks were truly awe-inspiring.

Cody cleared his throat. "You putting on weight, Raven?"

My face got hot. "You want me to push you off this rock?" I asked.

"Sorry," he said. "Just thought you'd like to know."

I stared at him, incredulous. "You thought I'd *like* to know? Why?"

He shrugged. "I was a dancer, remember? We had to be seven-percent body fat or less, and so if one of us was getting a little chunky, the others would point it out. Better than having the boss pull you aside, right? Professional courtesy. That's all."

I shook my head in disgust, even angrier because he was partly right. "You men can be so…robotic. Of *course* it makes sense, if you look at it rationally. But…"

"If I look at it like a woman?" Cody was smiling.

I put my hands on my hips. "Yes. For a damned minute, look at it like a woman. Like a human being. I *know* I'm plumping up, thank you. I do *not* want to be reminded of it. Got it?"

Cody pouted and turned away. "Got it," he muttered. I had probably been too hard on him, but *seriously*. Who tells a girl she's gaining weight? Especially if it's only like five pounds? Or a couple of kilograms?

"Let's get out of here," I said, grabbing his impossibly sculpted shoulder. He could easily have still been a dancer if he wanted, but unlike me, he didn't need the money.

On the way down the hill, he began pulling off his T-shirt, which was soaked with perspiration.

"Don't," I said.

"Why not?"

"It's too painful. The fact that you look like *that* and don't even like women? It's a crime against humanity. That's what it is. I don't need to see your abs again."

He sighed and left his shirt on. "If I liked women," he said, "you'd be at the top of my list. You're beautiful, okay? Forget about what I said."

Oh, so now he was pitying me. *Great.* I remained silent, but it was hard to stay mad at him. We headed out of the park, grabbed lunch, and then parted ways, but not before Cody could apologize sixteen more times. *Men.* The fact that he was so nice about it almost made it worse.

The next day, Dinesh called me up much too early for my taste. It had been a surprisingly busy Sunday night at Cougar's, so I hadn't gotten to sleep until after four. From what I could understand in my sleepy-headed, noncaffeinated state, the team was going to meet up at another off-Strip casino that evening. Dan had staked us with another ten grand based partly on our winnings from last time. I was instructed to dress like a tourist, whatever that meant. Tyler was going to play the role of my boyfriend, something I didn't completely object to.

Everything was going smoothly that night until I went on a bad run, losing a remarkable twelve hands in a row which nearly wiped out my stake. Luckily, my "boyfriend," Tyler, was able to spot me another three hundred, and he made sure to grumble about it as any real boyfriend would do. Among us, we finished the night up only six hundred bucks. We repaired to the nearest Denny's restaurant to lick our wounds.

"If we could make six hundred bucks every day, it would be pretty sweet," Tyler said. "But we only have a limited number of days before they catch on. So that's why it's important to win big and get out of there."

Dinesh was nodding. "Six hundred is basically a waste. There are only so many casinos around, and now we can't go back to this one for months."

"Without lots of crazy disguises, anyway," I said.

Dinesh smiled, patting the fake gut he was still wearing underneath his shirt. It made him look forty pounds heavier. "The disguises are just a crutch," he said. "We're trying to fool the human beings who might be watching us. But once they turn the facial recognition software on, none of it matters."

We went through the routine of signing the back of an envelope—much thinner than the first envelope—and Tyler promised to take it over to Dan. And then I was on my own.

On my drive home, I reflected on the situation. Without being able to physically observe the other players on my team, I wouldn't be able to guarantee that they weren't slipping some cash into their pockets without reporting it to the team as a whole. That was the weak link. By design, we played at different tables in order to cast as wide a net as possible, fishing for the elusive hot table. Even so, my sense of the other guys was that they were rooting for us as a team and that the thief, if there was one, wasn't in my own group.

I relayed my thoughts to Dan in a long-winded voicemail the next day, and he texted me back to say he would place me in another group at next Friday's meeting. I'd still have the problem of not being able to watch each individual player, but at least I could get a sense for how they operated and whether or not anything fishy was going on.

The rest of that week had me doing grunt work for a regional bank whose president, until recently, had been one of my most reliable lap dance customers. For a while, I had even agreed to give private dances to accommodate his schedule. He always tipped generously and behaved himself, so it had been a major bummer when he had to give me up. The way I looked at it (being a black belt in rationalization), I was letting him blow off a little steam and have a little bit of fantasy in his life without him crossing the line and having a full-blown affair. Not surprisingly, however, his wife hadn't seen it the same way, and so when she found out about his expensive little hobby, she went ballistic. Whether or not she'd cooled off by now, he'd seen me in the newspaper and decided to hire me to do some investigative work. I took it for granted that he hadn't told his wife about our little reunion.

The job was at least a little bit interesting. The bank was about to sign off on a large mortgage to an unmarried couple. They'd provided all the necessary paperwork and had solid credit, but my CEO friend said his underwriter had a "funny feeling" about them, that something wasn't on the level. So he wanted me to follow them around and see what made them tick. Did they actually go to the jobs they claimed they had? Did they have any weird hobbies or drug habits? That kind of thing.

It turned out they *did* have some interesting habits. For example, they'd neglected to mention on their application that the man, a thirty-six-year-old computer programmer, was interested in hydroponics, the practice of growing plants with only water and nutrients. Now, it was possible that the guy had a legitimate interest in botany, but it was equally possible that he was growing marijuana in his basement. When I examined the online photos of the house they were planning to buy, it started to come together. It had a huge unfinished basement and sat on a remote lot backing up into the hardscrabble and mountains. There was also a large rusty shed in the corner of the property. If I was going to manufacture drugs, that's where I'd do it. My banking friend was grateful for the information and paid me more than I'd billed. It was nice to have a new client.

# CHAPTER SEVEN

———

Friday night's meeting got off to a slow start. For one thing, Dan wasn't there yet. The rest of us were milling around awkwardly until the guy known as O noticed a box of toys in the corner. Inside, he found three tennis balls and began juggling them, first in a tight little circle and then in a more whimsical and lofty pattern nearly hitting the ceiling. It was amusing for a few seconds, but O seemed to think he was deserving of some sort of medal just because he could keep a couple of balls in the air. He seemed disappointed when our attention drifted after only a few seconds.

Laura soon joined us, followed quickly by Dan, who was panting again. Dan reported on the last week's efforts, which were better than in previous weeks but not enough to lift us out of a general funk. Our team had done the best of the three, but Dan noted that I had called in Dinesh with only a few hands left in the shoe, thus squandering what could have been a much bigger opportunity. He wasn't mean spirited about it but instead used it as a constructive reminder to everyone else.

Dan then announced that I would be joining a different team which consisted of "Jordan," the guy wearing nothing but Chicago sports attire, a pious-looking woman named Lisa, and a German guy with thinning blond hair named Ulrich. My greatest accomplishment of the evening would be to avoid horking down five slices of pizza during the pre-meal prayer. I bowed my head somberly and tried to look like my mind wasn't fixated on the imminent feast of pepperoni and cheese spread on top of a diabolically savory tomato sauce. But then I remembered that gluttony was a sin, and I figured thinking about food during a prayer was probably some kind of cardinal sin—a sin on steroids. For penance, I resolved not to grumble the next time my church took up a second collection.

My new team would be hitting a large new casino just off the Strip, only about a mile from my home. The plan was to do it Saturday beginning at seven. That would cut into my work time at Cougar's a little bit, but I was game.

Saturday found me with none of the butterflies and nerves that had plagued me the previous week. It wasn't that I had achieved grandmaster-level expertise in card counting—some of the others were using much more advanced counting techniques—but I was comfortable enough that I knew it was impossible for me to screw it up too badly. I arrived uncharacteristically late, which meant I was there only three minutes early, and prowled the tables without looking like I was prowling them. In private eye school, they'd stressed that acting like a dingbat (i.e., like a regular American) seemed to help in any kind of attempt at deception. So I whipped out my cell phone and began talking to some imaginary person while my attention was focused on the dealers and their tables.

The first one was a dud. A young dealer, probably from Malaysia, was ripping the cards out of the shoe with practiced abandon, *thwackking* them down on the table with almost blinding speed. *No thanks.* The guy next to him was a little better, but the table was full. The third table was the charmed one, luckily. The guy could have been fifty or seventy. I couldn't tell, but his hair was a shiny greasy white tinged with a yellowish hue that was either a remnant of a natural blond color or, more likely, a half century's residue of cigarette smoke. He seemed more interested in telling stories than in dealing cards. Just my kind of guy.

After waiting out the tail end of a shoe, I began winning instantly and somewhat dramatically. Splitting aces and drawing tens to get a pair of twenty-ones, doubling down and drawing twenty against a dealer's seventeen, and even drawing two natural blackjacks in a row. Unfortunately, it wasn't the kind of action I was looking for. All my great hands had drawn out lots of the good cards in the deck, so I knew the remainder of that shoe would be weak. And it was.

An hour passed with no rhyme or reason to the cards, no pattern that would cause me to change my own bets, much less to call in Jordan, our team's big better. A late run near ten o'clock got me back to even, but that was as high as I got for the night. It made sense. The house had an edge—that was why they offered the game in the first place—and if a player couldn't find any advantage, she was lucky to come out even, as I had.

Apparently, eating junk food was a time-honored tradition among card counters because Jordan and Ulrich all but demanded that we repair to an In-N-Out Burger to do a postmortem on our session. Not wanting to rock the boat, I didn't object, even though I had to get to Cougar's. And I had learned last time that it was indeed possible, and even *preferable*, to perform nearly-nude dance routines on a stomach full of french fries and burgers. I say preferable because I wasn't constantly tempted to have snacks during my breaks which meant I probably ended up eating less over the course of the evening. Not that my scale had noticed.

Lisa wasn't joining us for the novel reason that she had other interests that were more pressing, including her own family—a husband, three kids. To me, it seemed almost quaint, given the crowd I normally ran with—a Who's Who of ne'er-do-wells, no-goodniks, ex-strippers, bouncers, and lowlifes of all stripes. Not to mention lawyers.

Jordan was in a good mood. He'd had a nice little run and all on his own had won more than twelve hundred dollars. He regaled us with his big wins as though they were war stories, and he was the commanding general, taking obvious pride in his strategy and bet changes. Jordan's enthusiasm was contagious, enough so that I all but ruled him out as the source of any theft. If he'd wanted to skim a bunch off the top, it would have been simple enough to tell us he'd done merely *okay* instead of great. None of us would have been the wiser.

Ulrich had an *okay* time of it himself, up two seventy, and Lisa had reported a small loss. Our total profit was about fifteen hundred, but that wasn't nearly enough to put a dent in the team's deep hole. Four-digit evenings weren't going to cut it. We needed the big scores, when the big bettor could sit down and start making fifteen hundred a *hand* and play half a shoe that way. Even so, everyone seemed reasonably satisfied, and my guess was that by winning a small amount, they could at least say the team's overall problem didn't lie with *them*. According to Jordan, they'd had similar results throughout the past several months. Up a little, down a little less, profitable but without any big scores to boast about.

On my way out, Ulrich stopped me with a tap on the arm. He seemed flustered.

"Hi," he said in his accented English.

"Hi." We were staring at each other like seventh graders at a school dance.

"Um," he stammered. "Never mind."

I stifled a chuckle. I'd seen that look before. That look of *hmm, what do I do now?* He was trying to ask me out but had lost his nerve at the critical moment.

"No, what?" I asked, trying to sound as kind as possible. I wasn't going to say *yes,* but I was trying to help him get over his obvious nervousness.

"Well, it's just that…" he trailed off again.

*This was an especially bad case of nerves,* I thought. It was very sweet, not to mention flattering.

"Did you want to ask me something?" I asked, trying to make it as simple as possible.

"Not exactly," he said. "It's just that…" he looked down at the floor in embarrassment and then continued. "You have a french fry stuck to your chin."

# CHAPTER EIGHT

———

So far, I figured Dan had racked up about nine hundred bucks in fees without learning the first thing about the problem he'd hired me to investigate. I had managed to win myself a little money along the way, but it was becoming clear that our approach of "embedding" me in the various team units was not going to uncover some kind of smoking gun. The players I'd met all seemed like decent people—hell, they operated their team out of a *church*. Lisa was a little squirrely for my tastes, quiet but passive-aggressive and obviously not impressed with me in any significant way. But I wasn't there to make buddies. I was there to find a thief.

For the sake of completeness, Dan found an excuse to switch me to the final team of card counters, who I joined on Monday night at a sprawling casino out in the desert. The costumes were different, but the story was the same. We were posing as a group of bikers just passing through on the highway, which had given me an excuse to buy a black Harley-Davidson tank top I'd been coveting for months. It looked so good on me that I considered officially becoming a biker chick. How, I wondered, does a girl make that transition from nonbiker chick to biker chick? Is there an application process? Or do you just start wearing biker clothes and *declare* your new identity? I assume you'd start out at the poser level then graduate to wannabe, and ultimately, if you stuck with it long enough and wore enough leather, you would be taken into the fold. The beauty of it was that as a woman, I didn't need to buy a motorcycle. The downside, of course, was the danger of attracting biker dudes, the kind of guys who lived on beef jerky and unfiltered cigarettes and wore the same pair of jeans nineteen days in a row. *Ew.*

I'm not sure if people were buying our biker vibe or not, but no one seemed to take much notice of us, and we got out of there with twenty-eight hundred and change, another decent score. It just reaffirmed my belief that none of the players were skimming anything off their winnings. And if they were, it would be almost impossible to prove it without catching them in the act. But because we were almost always at different tables, I couldn't keep dibs on the other players very closely. My ability to assess them was limited to reading their body language when they turned in their winnings. If any of them was being dishonest, I couldn't tell.

"Kind of what I figured," Dan said. I'd called him to report my findings, such as they were.

"You figured?" I asked.

"Well, I didn't want to tip my hand right at the outset, or else, you know…" he trailed off.

"I'm not following."

He cleared his throat. "If I told you up front that I wasn't expecting you to find anything, then maybe you wouldn't work as hard. Not *you* personally, but just, you know, people in general."

I smiled. He was kind of paranoid, but it made a little sense. "I get it. No offense taken. So what exactly was the point of hiring me?"

"It's a first step. A preemptive strike, really. My real suspicion, actually, is that my wife is the one taking the money somehow. I can't confront her about it if it's just a hunch, of course. But if—"

I cut him off. "If you've already hired an investigator and checked out everyone else, you've got a leg to stand on."

"Yup, you got it," he said. "As soon as I bring this up, which I'm dreading, she's going to start pointing fingers at the players. So I want to be ready for that."

"It's *something*," I said. "But you know what she's going to say?"

"What?"

"She's gonna say, 'You believe that bimbo over your own wife?'"

He was silent for a second, and then I heard a sigh come through the line. "You're right, of course. But what else are we gonna do? Have everyone submit to a polygraph?"

"I know," I said, trying to sound reassuring. "This was a good idea, all things considered. I'm just trying to prepare you for the shitstorm that's about to blow through."

He coughed uncomfortably.

"Shit," I muttered, making matters worse. "Sorry about my language." I'd forgotten he was pretty churchy. I generally tried to watch my mouth around children, but it wasn't because I thought foul language was inherently evil or un-Christian. The Jesus I heard about in my own church was a long-haired dude who hung around prostitutes, fisherman, and lepers. Whenever you get that kind of crowd together, the language can tend towards the salty end of the spectrum.

"Anyway," he continued. "What do we do now?"

"She must keep books, right?" I asked.

"She does, but I don't know how helpful they'll be."

I thought for a second. "I'm pretty worthless, but I have a friend working on his MBA. He's got an accounting background. We could take a look for you."

"Probably a good idea," he said. "Same expectation, though. You're probably not going to find anything. But this way, we rule out any accounting snafus in advance."

"Another preemptive strike," I said.

"Bingo," he said, laughing. "I'll email you what I have, and you can ship it over to your friend. Thanks for the help, Raven."

I checked my watch. We'd been talking for about five minutes, but it wasn't worth the effort to mark it down and bill him for the time. I wasn't a lawyer, after all. It was probably too early in the morning to call Carlos, my quasi-accountant friend. He worked as a bouncer at Cougar's, but on the side, he was working towards his master's in business, and he owned a number of apartment buildings as well. If there was anything funny going on with the books, he'd be able to sniff it out.

Dan's email arrived soon after. He flattered me by thinking I'd have Microsoft Excel on my computer, which I didn't, but I was able to pull up the spreadsheets using free Google software. To me, it was all gobbledygook, a bunch of inputs, expenses, overhead, costs, and the like.

Although Carlos and I were friends, I had never emailed Carlos, so I'd have to wait until he woke up to call him. I gave him until noon and then called. Predictably, I woke him up, but he pretended not to mind.

"I had to get up soon anyway. It was rough last night. We had a fight. Carmine got his arm broken," he said.

"Wow, on a Monday night? Glad I missed it," I said.

"Yeah," he said, "two dudes wanted a dance from the same girl. You know how that goes."

"Huh," I muttered. "No one ever got in a fight over *me*."

Carlos sniffed. "I can't believe you're jealous. Anyway, what's going on?"

I filled him in. Carlos had worked with me as a freelancer a number of times, usually in the capacity of a muscle-bound intimidator or protector. This was the first time I was asking him to use his brain.

"Yeah, just send them over, and I'll take a look," he said. "It still sounds weird, though. A bunch of hyper-religious card counters?" He chuckled.

"Only in Vegas," I said.

He promised to get back to me by tomorrow. That afternoon he was busy taking his girlfriend's daughter to the movies and then out to dinner, but he said he'd be able to get to it eventually. Carlos had been dating the same woman for years, on and off, but he'd never hidden his interest in me. He had a great body, had commitment potential, and was great with kids. And he even made me laugh sometimes. But he was only about twenty-five, and I was, well, a little longer in the tooth than that.

Tuesdays were my Sundays, the lazy days when I futzed around with old records or CDs and sat out on my balcony getting a no-lines tan to the cool jazz stylings of Dizzy Gillespie or the warm tenor voice of José Carreras, the most underrated of the famed Three Tenors. It was also the day when I missed family life the most. I was still on reasonable terms with my sister, a veterinarian assistant in Illinois, but my parents had essentially written me off once they found out how I was paying my bills. I can't say I blamed them. It was only partly because I was a stripper—the rest of it was the web of lies I had told them over the years to cover it up. "I was a model," I said, "a high-roller hostess," and, "I worked at trade shows and publicity events." Some of which was true. My worst gig ever, even worse than any work I did with my clothes off, was working an international auto show. I was "the girl" standing on a rotating platform next to a Saab hatchback. I had to stand there and smile nonstop for stretches of up to two hours. Not being a naturally joyous and bubbly person, my facial muscles began to spasm, forcing me to massage my cheeks while dozens of passersby looked up at me and thought, *what's the deal with her???* My face hurt for weeks, and even now, I cringe any time I see a Saab on the road.

But by and large, my money had come from good old-fashioned nudity. That was where the money was, but it had several costs I hadn't considered at the outset. It cost me most of my close relationships and had prevented me from developing many new ones, with both men and women alike. Men only wanted one thing, and women looked at me as a sellout. Despite the fact that sex was everywhere in modern society, people still looked down upon people who made a living off it. Which was probably a good thing.

I didn't hear from Carlos that day or the next, but I knew he'd be working at the club with me on Wednesday night, so I didn't bug him about the little project I'd given him. After the first set at Cougar's, which ended around 10:15, he tapped me on the shoulder just as I was entering the employee lounge.

"You've got yourself into a pretty profitable group," he said. "At least, they *used* to be."

"I know. That's kind of the point," I said. "Anything jump out at you?"

"Little things here and there," he said. "For one, that lady keeps track of *everything*. I mean, if someone orders a Diet Coke during a meeting, it's recorded there. I wonder if they're trying to deduct it for tax purposes."

I nodded. "They said they were even deducting the pizza they ordered at meetings."

He shrugged. "They have to report the income, of course. But maybe they can deduct their expenses off the top. I don't know. I'm not a tax guy," he said.

"Okay, anything else?" I asked.

"They also have charitable contributions. Ten percent of their winnings goes straight to the church. Or, it *did*. When they had winnings."

"Got it," I said. "That doesn't surprise me since they're a pretty religious bunch. But I'm beginning to wonder if there's a deeper connection, though. You know—are these guys involved in church management somehow, or are they just regular members?"

"Something to look at, I guess," he said. "So," he said and then paused. A small grin crept across his face. I knew what was coming.

I put my hands on my hips. "How much?" I asked.

"Well, it was an hour and a half, and I charge more when I use my hard-earned business acumen, so—"

I guffawed, causing half the girls in the lounge to turn in our direction. "Your *business acumen*?"

He shrugged. "I bust my ass in all those accounting classes. And that wasn't really my thing, either. I'm more into the finance side of things."

*Here we go,* I thought. Carlos had a Donald Trump side to him, a penchant for waxing at length about his investing prowess and how smart he was. I wasn't in the mood.

"Okay, I'll give you a little extra this time," I said. "But the next time you utter the phrase 'business acumen,' I'm going to cut you off for good."

He pouted, but I knew he was pleased with himself. Carlos went back to work, and I got myself a Red Bull in preparation for a long night. Many of the top draws had skipped work that night which was common enough on Wednesdays, so that meant lots of lap dances for me, the customers apparently undeterred by my extra pounds.

# CHAPTER NINE

———

Thursday morning.

Mike Madsen was frowning at me.

"We'd split it fifty-fifty, of course," I said.

"And how much does this stuff cost?" he asked, his muscled forearms folded across his chest. Standing six foot one, he was a tower of skepticism.

"I don't know. I'll have to shop for it and everything. But let's say fifteen hundred bucks."

"Each?" he asked.

"Each," I said.

The good folks at the registration bureau in Carson City had randomly assigned Mike to supervise me during my first year as a PI. Recently, we also began sharing an office suite. To call the office an eyesore would be a disgrace to eyesores everywhere. It was a museum of dilapidated metal desks, 1970s furniture, and carpeting stained with Sanka and other fluids of unknown provenance. If I was going to make a go of this private eye thing, I had to do it my way. And that meant new furniture.

Mike was still hemming and hawing, oblivious of how impossibly cute he looked when he furrowed his brow. He was about my age, with blue-gray eyes, an athletic build, and the sandy-haired, clean-cut look of an NFL quarterback. We had hit it off, which is why we'd started sharing office space, but sometimes his Mormon sensibilities got in the way, clouding his mind with sound judgment and common sense. Every time we started to connect, I could sense danger signals going off somewhere in his subconscious. And he didn't even know about my night job.

I knew from Mike's continued silence that I'd won the battle, just as God intended.

"So?" I asked.

"Fine," he said, sighing dramatically. "But I don't want to do any shopping. You do everything, and just send me the bill."

"No problem there," I said, relieved. The notion of shopping for furniture with a man was mildly horrifying.

"But nothing, you know, *weird*," Mike said. "This is an office."

I smiled. "What were you expecting, zebra prints and purple velvet?"

He shrugged. "I don't know. It just makes me a little nervous. Especially for fifteen hundred bucks."

"Hey, you can deduct it," I said. "That means it's like it's on sale!"

"Yeah, that's exactly what it's like," he said, rolling his eyes. He turned to go back into his office.

"Anyway," I said, halting his escape. "I've got this thing I'm working. You ever hear of The Meadows Worship Center?"

He turned back to me and stared blankly. "No. Is it a church?"

"Yeah. It's a nondenominational Christian church about two miles from here. The weird part is, there's a group of card counters running a team out of there."

Mike cocked his head. "Only in Vegas," he said, chuckling.

I nodded. "Their angle is that they're morally opposed to gambling, so they try to stick it to the casinos by winning lots of their money. Then they turn around and give some of the winnings back to the church."

"That actually makes a little bit of sense," he said. "Maybe I should join them."

"Since when are you against gambling?"

He smiled. "Since I never win. So what's the job?"

"The head of the group thinks someone's stealing from them," I said. "Actually, he thinks it's his wife. She keeps the books." I filled him in on the rest. He was impressed that I could count cards without making a mess of things.

"I actually tried that a few times myself," he admitted. "Read a few books on it, even. But I couldn't quite keep up."

"It's like riding a bike," I said. "Once you get it, it just comes naturally."

Mike mumbled something unintelligible.

"What was that?" I asked.

He sighed. "I can't ride a bike, either." He folded his arms defensively and grimaced.

I felt my eyes getting big. "You never learned to ride a bike?"

"Yeah, yeah, long story. So how are you going to catch the wife?" He was suddenly eager to talk about something other than cycling.

I gave him a pass, but I filed that little tidbit away for safekeeping. "I don't know," I said. "My friend looked at the books, and there's nothing too unusual going on. The spreadsheets wouldn't tell us if she was taking something off the top, though, so that's not surprising. I'm just trying to see if there's some kind of deeper connection between the card-counting group and the church itself."

"And why is that?" Mike asked, leaning against his office door.

"Well, the books showed that they donated ten percent of their winnings to the church. Which I suppose isn't that unusual since they use the building for their meetings."

"Like a tithe," Mike said. "Ten percent is pretty standard. So why not join the church? That's the best way to get on the inside."

I cringed. "I'm already pretending to be a real member of the card-counting team. But it's something else to join a church under false pretenses."

Mike smiled. "You think God would mind?"

I shrugged. "I suppose he has better things to worry about. Like that awful shirt you're wearing, for example."

Mike pretended to be offended, but he knew that his short-sleeved khaki shirt was indefensible.

I decided to press the point. "Is that from Goodwill or the Salvation Army? I can't tell."

"I don't really do much shopping, so I have no idea," he said lamely.

I shook my head. It was a losing battle, like trying to convince Donald Trump to get a haircut. I took my leave of Mike, happy to get his agreement, or at least acquiescence, in the need to buy new office furniture.

My next step was to figure out if Laura Hartman was stealing from the group. I was stumped as to how to go about proving it since it was such a private crime. After all, she collected all the money and then reported how much was there. Apart from catching her in the act, which seemed unlikely, there was no way to actually witness the deed.

But gradually, as I paced around my little office, a plan began coming together. Even if I couldn't prove the *how* of the theft, I might be able to prove the *why*. Every thief had a reason for stealing, whether it was drugs or just plain greed, and if I could uncover Laura's reason, it might unravel the whole mystery.

I didn't know her very well yet, but she didn't give the impression of being overly interested in material goods, and so I had little hope of uncovering a hidden cache of Prada handbags and Jimmy Choo shoes or a secret garage stuffed with Ferraris. In short, apart from the missing money, there were no red flags.

I sighed and looked out my window down at a homeless man digging into an improbably large takeout lunch. It was beginning to dawn on me that this job would never be easy. If a problem was easy, the client wouldn't go through all the hassle and expense of hiring a private investigator. They only came to us with the tough ones, the problems whose solutions didn't immediately jump right out at you. The best I could hope for was to do a better job of staying out of danger.

After lunch, I found Dan and Laura's address and drove over to their house, a midsized ranch home perched on a wide lot with colorful desert stones blanketing the yard. A small dog, unleashed, was wandering around and sniffing at the trees. Like many Nevada homes, there was a carport instead of a garage. This one was empty.

I was a little unclear what Dan's expectations were. Obviously, he knew I would be investigating his wife, but I wondered whether or not he wanted me poking around his homestead and digging into her personal life. As I was gazing at their spread, a shadow crossed in front of the left window, and then a form appeared at the door. It appeared to be a teenaged girl, probably their daughter. She opened the door and then whistled at the dog which proceeded to ignore her. She put her hands on her hips, whistled again, and then yelled at the dog whose name was Sparky.

I could *see* her whole body sigh, as though she was saying "Here we go again," and then she stormed out and gave poor Sparky the business which involved some sharp scolding and a little chase before she snatched the little pooch up and brought him inside. The girl was tall, long-legged, and anywhere between fifteen and eighteen, pretty despite being garbed only in a tank top and pajama bottoms. Was she skipping school, I wondered? It was around noon on a Thursday in September, which had me curious.

Apart from the girl's presence, there was nothing unusual about the house which was situated in a quiet neighborhood of similar ranches that predated the more recent housing boom's love affair with two-story cookie-cutter homes. The visit didn't tell me very much except to confirm that Laura wasn't living high on the hog. At least, she didn't *appear* to be.

With that bit of almost useless information under my belt, I moved on. I'd have to connect with Dan to find out more about Laura—where she worked, shopped, and that kind of thing—and if there were any boundaries I should not cross. After all, I was investigating his own wife, the mother of his children.

That afternoon I got another call from my bank president friend, who had another job lined up for me. Supposedly, he thought one of his best loan officers was being courted by another regional bank, and he wanted me to confirm that before he committed to promoting the guy. I couldn't help feeling that he was using my new job as an excuse to see me. Eighty percent of me felt bad for his wife, but the other twenty was flattered. It wasn't like I was going to sleep with the guy. I was just going to play a small role in whatever little fantasy he was trying to live out. The fact that he always paid well, and in cash, had *nothing* to do with it. Rationalization 1, Truth 0.

# CHAPTER TEN

———

On Friday morning, I woke to an email from Dan which answered most of my questions. Surprisingly, he said there were no boundaries. Nothing was off-limits. I should follow the money, Woodward and Bernstein style, wherever it led. He also gave me some basic information about his wife. She worked part time at a local gambling software company (another delicious irony), golfed in a ladies' league on Monday mornings, and belonged to the Desert Athletic Club where she did Pilates and played tennis. That explained why she was in such great shape. Though sparse, the information was enough to get me started. I responded and asked him about their family, something I'd forgotten to mention in the first email. I also thought about asking him if he knew any of her passwords so I could check her email, but I wasn't quite ready to take that step. Even though Dan had said there were no boundaries, hacking emails was a whole different level of snooping.

Leftover pizza and orange juice made a splendid breakfast on my balcony, which by eleven had warmed up considerably. Pizza for breakfast was one of my most treasured benefits of single life. I couldn't imagine being able to get away with such a thing with a husband and kids around. First of all, there wouldn't *be* any pizza leftovers. And second, even if there were, they'd scarf them down before I ever got my paws on them.

I knew I needed a plan to begin understanding what made Laura tick. Without prompting, Dan had said he'd cut me a new check to cover additional hours on the project, so I viewed that as a green light to start digging. In my brief months working as a private investigator, I had uncovered some of the most unusual things just by watching and paying attention, trying to keep out of sight and stay out of trouble.

After breakfast, I rang up the valet and told him to have my Porsche ready to go. For eighty bucks a month, my building offered valet services, which it had done since before I moved in. But the most recent improvement was a policy change *forbidding*, not just discouraging, tips. Instead, the valets would now receive a standardized percentage of the overall valet fees. This had "opened the door" for me to use their service much more often. Even though I worked for tips myself, I didn't regard driving a car for two minutes and holding the door open for me as a service worth five bucks, and evidently neither did most of the other residents in my building. But since the new antitip policy came into effect, half the residents had signed up, and the valets were busier than ever. And probably richer, too.

Tommy, my favorite valet, wasn't working this shift, but there was a new guy who filled in nicely. Martin, a tall transplant from somewhere in eastern Europe, had a toothy grin that made his cheeks dimple, which was the surest way to get me to melt.

"Nice car," he said, holding the door open.

I soon realized Martin needed some additional training, including a stern lecture about adjusting the car owner's seat position. He'd moved the seat so far back that I could barely reach the pedals. After pointedly readjusting the seat and flashing him a thin smile, I sped off and headed over to Dan and Laura's house to do a drive-by.

When I arrived, just after eleven o'clock, a tiny silver SUV was parked in the carport. There was no sign of a teenage girl or a dog. I drove slowly past the house and then parked up the street next to a lot where a house was being constructed. I would hang out for a while to see if anything happened and then move on. From my limited experience, I knew these things were hit-or-miss. You could watch someone for a week and not see anything, or you could learn the universe about a guy in ten minutes. The problem was, there was no way to tell in advance.

Luckily, I was charging by the hour because there was nothing going on at Dan's house. I had brought a *Glamour* magazine with me to pass the time, but I'd breezed through it in forty-five minutes. Next time, I'd pack a Russian novel. I knew

Dan would be out at his day job as a computer programmer, so I'd figured it would be a good time to catch Laura on her own, possibly with her guard down. But after more than an hour, I was convinced she might just be staying in for the day. It was well past noon, and I was getting hungry.

I gave it ten more minutes and then drove back out of the subdivision, the whole way home resisting the urge to stop and grab some fast food. I knew I had the makings for a megasalad in my fridge, and I wasn't going to let the lettuce wilt away like I usually did.

I was out of shredded cheese, so I had to hunt down the cheese grater. After all, you couldn't have a proper salad without cheese. And hardboiled eggs. And walnuts. And ranch dressing. And croutons. And before I knew it, I found myself scarfing down what was probably the calorie equivalent of a Double Whopper and fries. I felt a little bit guilty about it but not much, reasoning that calories weren't everything. My lunch was much healthier than fast food. At least, until I cut myself a few extra slices of cheese as I cleaned up after myself.

That left the rest of the afternoon. I had a two o'clock meeting with Alex, my bank president client, strategically located at a Starbucks across the street from his bank headquarters. Apparently, I wasn't the kind of business relationship he wanted clicking her heels across the bank's gleaming marble floors, but I didn't take too much offense. I knew my place. I was a forbidden, naughty treat, something to be kept hidden away from the other employees, a bunch of nosey functionaries who might get ideas and report them to Alex's pesky wife. The funny part was that Alex was such a gentleman there was never a chance that any funny business would go on. And of course, I wasn't exactly the kind of girl who'd get down and dirty on the boardroom table in the middle of the afternoon. At least, not without a few martinis in me.

Alex was early. He looked drawn, tired, thinner. Always trim and athletic, he now seemed a little too skinny, borderline gaunt, as he stood to greet me. Late forties with a full head of slowly graying black hair, he was dressed in the classic executive "casual Friday" golf shirt and khakis, a brown belt cinched an extra knot tighter around his waist. Unconsciously, I said a quick and silent prayer that he wasn't ill.

"Alex, *hi*," I beamed, trying to mask my dismay at his appearance.

Ever gallant, he pulled out a stool for me to sit on.

"Great to see you again, Raven," he said. "What are you drinking?"

"I'm not into any of those coffee concoctions," I said. "I take it black and boring."

He smiled. "Same here. I'll be right back."

I didn't even bother to protest, knowing he'd take it as an insult if I tried to pay my way. I'd forgotten exactly where he was originally from—Tennessee, North Carolina, something like that—but wherever it was, it was somewhere I needed to spend a few months. Most men didn't get how utterly and embarrassingly *easy* it was to treat a lady right, but some of these Southern types had it down *cold*. And Alex was as cool as they came.

"Here you go," he said, placing a giant cup of steaming coffee in front of me.

I sniffed. "Alex, if I drink that whole thing, I'll have a heart attack!"

He shrugged. "I didn't know what size to get," he said awkwardly. "We've never had coffee before."

I slurped at the piping hot coffee and decided to get down to business. "Your man *is* thinking about leaving the bank," I began. I hadn't done a whole bunch of investigating, to be honest. But Alex would understand. The investigation was just a formality, a bogus excuse to get together with me.

He perked up. "How can you tell?"

"Well, it's not much, actually. I haven't tailed him or anything. But I noticed that he updated his LinkedIn page recently. It's almost like a formal résumé, which is unusual for someone who's worked at your company for...how long?"

"Nine years," he said resignedly. He was staring down into his coffee.

"You seem distracted," I said, choosing my words carefully.

He offered a weak smile and then looked plaintively out the window. "She's leaving me, Raven. After almost twenty years."

I almost choked on my coffee. "Pamela?"

"Yes, Pamela," he sighed. "I haven't been eating. Not sleeping. I'm sure I look awful. You know what's funny about it?"

"What?" I asked, relieved that he wasn't sick.

He winced before speaking. "She's using *you* as an excuse. It's a joke, of course, but she thinks it'll mean a bigger divorce settlement."

My eyes got big. "She's divorcing you because you went to a strip club?"

"It was my fault, I guess. I shouldn't have been so honest with her. But when she found out, I panicked. So I told her that I'd seen you once, twice a week for years. So it wasn't just going to a strip club. She felt like I was cheating on her, basically. And of course, she exaggerates everything in her mind."

I kept quiet and slurped at my piping hot coffee. In private lap dances, especially with good customers, dancers made sure that the "dance" was not just visual but tactile as well. Customers could not touch with their hands, but the dancer would spend a fair amount of effort pressing her thighs onto the customer and occasionally brushing against a customer's face. But Alex, ever the gentleman, had just wanted to look at me. He would sit in the chair, and I would stand up, facing him from about five feet away. He often wore a kind of goofy *aww shucks* grin on his face, a remnant of his rural southern upbringing. Recalling his face made me smile involuntarily.

Alex looked at me quizzically.

"Sorry," I said. "I was just thinking of something."

"So was I," he said, looking at me intently.

Our eyes locked, and something inside me quivered. Alex had dark-brown eyes, almost black, and at that moment, they were burning with an intensity I'd not seen in any of our countless meetings. They seemed almost to be boring through me, but instead of making me uncomfortable, they lit a fire in the core of my abdomen. Alex was a powerful man, a president of a bank with branches in three states, and at that moment, I felt a glimmer of the power that had driven him to the top.

"Raven," he began softly.

I knew what he was going to suggest. That it didn't have to be a fantasy anymore. That he was a free man now, and we could start something bigger and a million times more meaningful. My heart was thumping in my chest in a way it hadn't in a long time. Then again, maybe he was just going to tell me that I had a french fry stuck to my face.

I shifted in my seat. "Alex," I whispered, "let's take this very slowly, all right?" Some deep-seated and ancient panic had kicked in, warning bells going off for reasons I couldn't fully explain.

He leaned back in his chair, eyes fixed now on his hands, which were cupped around his tall coffee. His gold wedding ring remained on his ring finger, I noticed. When he looked up, his eyes were no longer smoldering and intense but kindly and understanding.

"I get it," he said, forcing a light chuckle. "I'm old."

I shook my head vigorously. "No, not at all. Let's just…" I was fumbling for words.

"Get back to business?" he asked, trying to be helpful.

Given his imminent divorce, Alex had probably expected to be the one to be pitied, but now he was the one taking pity on me. For reasons I still couldn't explain, I had turned a moment of passion between two adults into an avalanche of awkwardness. I took a deep breath and tried to smile.

"So is there anything else you want me to do about your wayward employee? Is he that good?"

Alex straightened up and looked out the window for a moment. "He's worth saving, yes. I think you can leave him alone, though. We don't need to go stalking him around town or poring through his trash. I'll just come up with a reason to give him a promotion. Hopefully, that'll keep him."

"Okay," I said, grateful to be back to business talk.

He sipped at his coffee and then smiled. "But if you need to pad the bill a little more, that's fine too. I'm the one signing off on the expense reports."

I shrugged. "We'll see. I'm actually pretty busy with some other projects."

"That's very good to hear," he said, perking up. "You know," he confided in a low voice, "I never liked the idea of you dancing for other men. I mean, obviously, that was your job, but it just didn't sit well with me."

*Back to the personal stuff*, I thought, cringing. I decided to go with the flow since it couldn't be any more awkward than my attempts to avoid it. "And why didn't it sit well?"

Alex peered out the window again, his thoughts a world away. And then he turned back and faced me, his expression earnest. "Because, Raven, you're perfect. I sometimes wished I had a talent for art because I would have quit my job and devoted myself to trying to capture your image, painting you over and over again so that God's perfection would never be lost. The way your cheekbones jut out at the perfect spot"—he began gesturing at my face—"the way your lips have a soft pout to them, the way your eyebrows perfectly frame your stunning eyes. I could go on and on. The point is, I don't think most people got that about you. Men focus on your body and its obvious attractions, but they miss the fact that you're *art*, a piece of walking, talking art. Even your voice…" he trailed off and looked out the window again.

My face had turned into an inferno from the tips of my ears down through my neck and into my chest. In all my life, I'd never been spoken to like that, and I had no idea how to process it. Again, my first instinct was to *flee*, to run away from such feeling, such intensity, the kind of passion I craved but knew I didn't deserve. But I stayed put.

"Alex, that's so kind," I whispered, still blushing furiously.

"Yes, well," he said softly, tailing off. He might have gotten a bit carried away, and now he was blushing a bit himself. But at least I knew where he stood, and I had no doubt about where I stood with him. He leaned in to peck me on the cheek, and we parted ways soon after, pretending as though nothing much had happened, but of course it had. I danced at my club for about four hours and then spent a mostly sleepless night drifting in and out of bizarre dreams, many of which were about Alex.

# CHAPTER ELEVEN

———

Saturday mornings had a way of going by too fast, aided by the simple fact that I usually woke up around eleven after a late night at Cougar's. Dan had left a text on my phone telling me that his wife was going to the gym after lunch, whatever "after lunch" meant, so I fixed myself a quick brunch consisting of what I called a pizza omelet. Italian sausage, peppers, mozzarella cheese, and tomato sauce, onions, and a few eggs, all thrown together in the pan and flipped a half-dozen times. I couldn't resist frying up some shredded potatoes and dousing them in olive oil and salt and pepper. That would keep me going all day, I figured.

I slid into some gym attire and called down for my car and headed over to Dan's house where I hoped to catch Laura on her way out. Her car was still in the driveway when I pulled up, so I drove past the house and parked at the same construction site I'd been to the previous day, fixing their driveway in my rearview mirror.

It didn't take as long as I'd feared before Laura's car emerged and crept backwards down their driveway. I slowly did a U-turn and kept my distance to a healthy two hundred yards behind her. I already knew she was headed to the gym, so I wasn't overly concerned about losing her.

I was wrong. Within a minute of starting up my engine, I knew she wasn't headed to the gym. The gym was west, and she was heading in a decidedly northeast direction. The weird part was that she'd made a westerly turn out of her subdivision but then had circled back to go almost in the opposite direction, almost as though she suspected Dan might be watching her as she pulled out. I decided to ease off the gas just in case she was being extra paranoid.

Eventually, we got caught up at the same stoplight, which caused me to rethink my flashy Porsche. It was the kind of car someone being tailed might notice, I realized, and if she noticed it, she might remember it, too. But Laura seemed perfectly oblivious to me, though, so I continued behind her and eased off the pedal to let a sanitation truck come between us. We were headed into a not so great part of town. Not quite sketchy but not the kind of place a fashionable and fit supermom like Laura would be comfortable.

And then it hit me. She must be headed to their church. That was the only reason she'd be driving where she was, and my suspicion was confirmed a few minutes later when she slowed and turned into the church parking lot. There was no way I could pull in behind her because I would stick out too obviously in the otherwise empty lot. Instead, I continued driving and planned to circle around a few minutes later.

When I came back a second time, her car wasn't visible from the main drag, so I eased my Porsche into the main parking lot and slowly crept around the various buildings on the church property. In addition to the church proper, where I'd never set foot, there was the annex in which we had our team meetings. Attached to that building was a small residence that jutted off in an L-shape, and it was there that I found Laura's car. It was parked in a small driveway next to the house, alongside a late model BMW sedan.

A secret rendezvous...at church? Was Laura involved with the minister? I didn't know much about him except for the fact that the billboard out front said his name was the Rev. Owen Clavette. Was the Rev engaging in some personal ministry with my client's wife? And if so, did that have anything to do with the missing money?

I drove by slowly, careful to keep my car's engine from making too much noise. I drove back to the main lot and wound through a driveway to a check-cashing store, where I parked. Walking back to the pastor's house, I realized it was a gamble. I had no plausible reason for being there, so if they spotted me, my cover would most likely be blown. But I wanted to get closer, to try to tease out what was actually going on. Simply parking at someone's house didn't mean anything nefarious was going on. They could have been playing Parcheesi for all I knew. But then, why the deception?

I snuck up next to the house without being seen. Naturally, the windows were all shut tight, probably hadn't been opened since April, and the curtains were drawn. The air conditioner hummed along loudly, dimming my hopes of hearing anything inside. I moved as close as I could to the window facing the church parking lot, hoping no other interlopers would arrive and wonder what the skanky woman in gym attire was doing creeping around the pastor's house. By design, probably, the lot remained deserted. I figured Laura and Owen had probably chosen this time precisely because no one would have any business at the church on a Saturday around lunchtime. There were no meetings, no prayer groups, no child care, and no mass until five o'clock. It was the perfect time for a private get-together.

I had no luck next to the other window, either. The noise from the air conditioner wasn't as bad, but unless the people inside the house started screaming, I wasn't going to hear anything over its annoying whirr. Frustrated, I whipped out my phone and snapped a few photos of Laura's car parked at the house. I made sure to time stamp them, just to drive the point home. Laura was with another man at exactly the same time she'd told her husband she would be at the gym. It was the perfect crime, I realized. Dan, a soft man comfortable in his corpulence, was more likely to get struck by lightning than set foot in a gym, so Laura's cover story gave her a blank check to do whatever she wanted. Dan would never be the wiser.

Satisfied with a few photos stored on my phone, I did a quick walk back to my car and got out of there before my luck changed. I spent the rest of the afternoon wondering whether or not I could avoid telling Dan about what I'd found. He'd hired me to look into missing money, not to see if his wife was having an affair. But since the affair could be all tied up with the money, it was certainly a relevant fact to report. But I wasn't going to do it that day. I was going to work myself up to it. By shopping.

After lunch, I found myself braving the heat and strolling down to the Fashion Show Mall where most of the employees in the Nordstrom shoe department knew me by name. Over the years, I'd convinced myself that I didn't have a shopping problem because I only owned about thirty pairs of shoes, which meant most of the time I *didn't* buy any. Half the ones I bought, especially if I'd had a glass of wine beforehand, I returned to the store, no questions asked. And some of the other ones I'd even sold on eBay, often getting more than a hundred bucks a pair. So I was no hoarder, no reckless spender of ill-gotten money, but just a girl who liked to keep her feet reasonably happy.

But I wasn't fully in the mood, it turned out, and walked out of there without any bags dangling from my arms. I was still bothered by the problem of Laura and the minister when a crazy idea popped into my head. While baking in the sun at a stoplight, I whipped out my phone and dialed my bouncer-MBA friend Carlos.

"Want to go to church?" I asked.

*Silence.*

"It's for a job. I need to check out the pastor," I explained.

"No," he said simply.

"You didn't even ask when or where or how much," I pointed out.

"My girlfriend has this thing, you know," he said.

"About me?"

"Yes, about you. She thinks I like you."

I chuckled. "Well, you do. So what? Are you married? Do you have a spine?" The light turned green, so I walked and taunted. "Tell her I need you. She's got to know there's no funny business going on, right?"

"There's not?" he shot back. He was referring to a night a few weeks earlier when I'd invited him up to my apartment for a late-night visit that I'd sorely needed at the time.

"Just tell her," I said insistently, studiously ignoring his question.

His sigh was audible even over the heavy Saturday afternoon Strip traffic. "Ok," he started. "Where and what time?"

"Tonight, five o'clock. At The Meadows Worship Center. You can pick me up," I said, cheerfully.

I could almost *hear* his eyes rolling, but he restrained himself and wisely kept his mouth shut. There was some kibitzing in the background, and then he got back on the line. "She said it's all right, but you have to start paying me more."

Now it was my turn to sigh. He'd fooled me, albeit briefly, into thinking that something other than money was the issue. "No way man, I'm paying you too much as it is. I have other people I can call," I bluffed.

"Like who?"

"Like the other PI I work with. He's got bigger muscles than you," I taunted, not exactly truthfully. "And you think Ryan wouldn't kill to come along with me?"

"Ryan from work?" He asked.

"Yes. He's been pestering me for weeks," I said, not exactly truthfully. Ryan had jumped into my head because he was *my* favorite bouncer, not because I was his favorite dancer.

Silence ensued.

"You there?" I asked.

"Yeah. I can't do it. Go ahead and call Ryan," he said.

My face flushed a deep color of red, the way an amateur poker player looks when his bluff has unexpectedly been called.

"Um, okay," I said softly, dumbfounded. "I will. I've got his number right here," I lied again. "Have a great afternoon with what's her name."

"Sofia," he muttered. "Later."

The line went dead as I turned west to get to my condo. *Wow*, I thought. I had always assumed that I basically *owned* Carlos, that he would answer to my beck and call on a moment's notice due solely to his unnatural interest in my body. He had never made any secret about his lust for me, but I guess I had taken him for granted.

Or not. My phone, still in hand, buzzed insistently.

"I'll pick you up at 4:30," said a resigned voice.

"Perfect," I said, stifling my glee. I didn't want to rub it in his face because calling me back must have been one of the hardest calls he'd ever made. Lust conquers all.

# CHAPTER TWELVE

————

Carlos was early, so I invited him up.

"This is too nice for you," he said matter-of-factly. The last time he'd been up here, he hadn't noticed a thing. "You must make more in tips than I thought!" He was staring out my floor-to-ceilings at the Strip a few blocks away. After shaking his head in mock disgust, he started meandering towards my bedroom.

I coughed loudly, signaling he shouldn't proceed.

"Whatever," he muttered, giving me the *you crazy* look. "You have any food?"

"Sofia doesn't feed you?"

He frowned. "I'm the cook, actually. And I don't *live* with her, either. We just, you know, hang out a lot."

"Um hmm," I said. "I might have something in the fridge."

Too late, I realized my fridge was a veritable museum of junk food, most of it classics from the eighties.

"You really eat this stuff?" Carlos asked, holding up a can of Cheez Whiz.

"It's just for parties," I said, shifting on my heels. "You know, you spray some on a Ritz and put a jalapeno on top. Easy as pie." I wasn't about to tell him that I'd sometimes make myself Cheez Whiz and turkey sandwiches. With sauerkraut, on a pretzel bun.

Now he was fondling my oversized jar of dill pickles. "You know that a single pickle has an entire day's supply of sodium?" He was beginning to sound like a twit.

"Put those back," I ordered. "Don't be bad-mouthing pickles in my kitchen."

Now he was on to the mayonnaise, holding up two squeeze bottles of regular and spicy. "What does *this* go on?"

"Never mind," I said, slamming the fridge door. "You want a rice cake to snack on? Well, I don't have any. You want a kale salad? I'm all out. You want goji berries? I don't even know what color those are. So it's Cheez Whiz or a pickle. Take your pick."

Naturally, I momentarily entertained the idea of putting Cheez Whiz *on* a pickle. I filed that away for future reference.

"Nah, I'm good," he said, looking somewhat frightened. "Let's get to church."

When we got downstairs, Tommy the valet gave Carlos the once-over and then fixed me with a quizzical look which I interpreted as amazement that a bimbo like me would actually be in the company of a well-built young man on a Saturday night. Granted, it was only four thirty in the afternoon, but still.

Carlos put his jet-black, stick shift Mustang into gear and pulled out loudly, probably charmingly unaware that his car would fail to impress the valets who were standing around scratching their butts. They were used to Bentleys and Benzes with the occasional Porsche or Audi thrown in. American-made cars were a curiosity at best.

I gave Carlos directions, and we made our way through thin traffic down to the sketchy neighborhood where the church was located.

"I've got a building just up that street," Carlos said, pointing. He was something of a wannabe real estate mogul, working on his MBA at UNLV by day while he worked as a bouncer by night. And somehow, he'd saved up enough cash to buy a few apartment buildings along the way.

"You have a lot of slum properties?" I asked indelicately.

He sniffed. "This ain't no slum," he said, butchering his grammar for effect. "You want to see a slum? I'll show you the first place I bought. Most of the renters pay by the week. It's more of a hotel than anything else."

I shrugged, not wanting to get him started. Apart from the size of his biceps, real estate was his favorite topic of conversation. I liked the guy more than I let on, and I found his ambition sexy, but I would have been more interested in discussing dental tape or tax accounting than apartment buildings.

We pulled into the church's lot, which was about half full. A surprising diversity of parishioners were making their way into the church—Koreans, Latinos, a few people who looked African, and a spate of boring white folks. The one thing they had in common was that they looked unusually happy to be there.

We got inside and were immediately pounced on by a bubbly young African woman named Korangi, who's somehow managed to encapsulate her life story into about thirty seconds of heavily accented English. I wasn't sure how she knew we were new to the church, but she did. She solemnly pressed pamphlets into our hands and gave us both hugs.

Before we could utter more than a peep, Korangi waved over a tall, older man who was also beaming. He was balding and had the look of a college professor, with a graying ponytail and spectacles, except that he was dressed in khakis, like an archeologist.

"More victims," he joked, his eyes dancing across our faces. "My name's Paul. Come. Follow me." Ever the cynic, I wondered how many times he had jokingly referred to newbies as "victims."

Paul led us through a thickening throng of people who were milling about in the rear of the church. We headed down a long corridor which then took us right into the wide open amphitheater-like church. It was bigger inside than it looked from the outside. A dozen or so immense columns held up the ceiling which soared thirty or more feet above us, cresting in countless peaks that all drew the eye towards a fresco of Jesus dying on the cross which adorned the ceiling across the front one-third of the church.

Paul showed us to a special section that was cordoned off by a gold colored rope.

"This is the VIP section," he smirked, no doubt recycling another joke. "When mass gets started, you'll see why." Paul's eyes were twinkling. He shook our hands, welcomed us again, and then left us alone.

There was a couple in front of us who was busying themselves by tending to their infant girl and making cooing noises at her. They couldn't have been happier to be there.

I elbowed Carlos. "Is this some sort of cult, you think?" I whispered.

He frowned. "What makes you say that?"

"Well, everyone's so…*friendly*. It can't be real."

"I thought you were religious," he said.

"I am. But not like *this*. It's more of a private thing with me," I explained.

"Whatever," he said. "People are different. My mom's church is a lot like this. They keep trying to get me to join."

"And why don't you?" I asked.

"I might, someday. Good way to make business connections."

I elbowed him again, this time, more firmly. "You're going to go straight to hell," I hissed.

He chuckled out loud, causing the dad in front of us to look up. "And you're *not*?" Carlos whispered.

He had a point. We sat in silence for another five minutes or so, at which point the lights dimmed and came back on, like at a play or symphony. And then the lights dimmed and stayed low. That got the increasingly large crowd to hush with an expectant buzz rippling throughout the room, and then the music started. It wasn't an organ but a concert grand piano elevated on the stage and highlighted by a half-dozen spotlights, played by an impossibly beautiful brunette of about eighteen. Soon enough some drums joined in, illuminated by a single spotlight, and this went on for another few minutes, the drums backing up the pianist but staying out of her way. A bass guitar then a lead guitar, and then two dozen members of the choir, previously unseen, suddenly began glowing under yet another spotlight as they joined in, their bright-blue gowns iridescent under the glare.

I had to admit, it was quite a show. We were all standing up, almost involuntarily swaying to the music, which got more and more feverish until finally, the man of the hour showed up. Like a boxer entering the ring, the Reverend Owen Clavette stalked down the main aisle from a previously invisible location in the rear of the church, shaking hands with some parishioners on the aisles and fist-bumping others. His face was all smiles, his teeth gleaming, the part in his hair so crisp that he must have used a ruler, and his face, dimples and all, had a ruddy glow to it, highlighted by the spotlight that followed him down the aisle. His gray suit was immaculately tailored to his athletic if not shortish body.

The stage was empty apart from a stool with a glass of ice water perched on it, almost like Clavette was going to do a stand-up routine. Even a cynic like me was looking forward to hearing what this guy had to say, that is if he ever made it up there. He was still bogged down in the aisle, fist-bumping and high-fiving parishioners, almost like a president walking into the congressional chamber to deliver a State of the Union address.

"This is nuts," Carlos murmured. He was ice-cold, not buying it.

"I kind of like it," I admitted. "I mean, check out that guy's suit! It's glistening. Probably silk mixed with some high-end cotton."

Carlos craned his neck around to look again.

"You just like him because…" he trailed off.

"He's *hot*?" I asked.

He shrugged. "Whatever."

"Never seen a hot reverend before," I admitted. "But you got me." As he finally made his way up to the stage—it was hardly an altar, as I understood the term—I couldn't help admiring his TV-anchor looks. He took a sip of water and scanned the crowd, which I estimated to be somewhere around eight hundred. The ambient lights slowly brightened but not so much so that there was any doubt as to who was the star of the show. The spotlight remained on the reverend, keeping up with him as he paced back and forth with the pent-up energy of a caged tiger, still remaining silent.

It was an old trick, I knew. The Romans had done it. Countless politicians and entertainers had done it. Even Hitler had done it, often arriving an hour or more late to his own rallies just to get the crowd into a state of rabid anticipation. And now Owen Clavette was doing it, pacing around, looking thoughtful, gazing out at the crowd but not saying a word.

A buzz started near the rear, and it quickly spread.

"What are they saying?" Carlos asked.

"I have no idea."

As it got louder, I could tell that the chant had a long *e* in it, but that was it.

"Breathe," Carlos said.

"I am."

He elbowed me. "No, I mean they're saying 'breathe'."

"Why?" I asked.

He shrugged.

I looked up and caught Clavette looking down at us, the members of the "VIP" section, seeing if the chant, seemingly spontaneous, had any effect on us. I tried to act duly impressed.

The whole crowd was into it now, and Clavette began stalking back and forth on the stage, lifting his hand to his ear, begging the crowd for more.

"*Breeeeathe!*" they said, almost in unison, repeating the word over and over in response to the minister's encouragement.

"Louder!" he demanded.

"*Breeeeeeeathe!*"

"Louder! So the Lord can hear you!"

"*Breeeeeeeeeeathe!*" they cried. I looked around and saw a few tears on people's faces. Many had planned ahead and held handkerchiefs in their hands.

"Once more!" he bellowed.

"*Breeeeeeeeeeeeeeathe!*" the crowd groaned, deeper this time.

"Let us all breeeeeeeeeathe!" Clavette bellowed. "Breathe *in* the word of Jesus. Breathe *out* the temptations of the dark one!'

"*Breeeeeeeathe!*" the crowd rejoined.

"Let us all breathe *in* the good works of our neighbor, and breathe *out* the lies of Satan!"

"*Breeeeeeathe!*" once more. The pitch was frenzied.

"Let us all breathe *in* the kind words of strangers, and breathe *out* the taunts of our enemies!"

The music started up again, beginning with the bass drum and then the bass guitar, aiding the crowd in reaching its preservice climax. The reverend was sweating already, looking serious and almost possessed by a higher power, a mission to cast out demons and save souls. He seemed to have the weight of the parish on his shoulders.

The choir started up again, and the reverend began whipping up the musicians, cajoling them to play louder and with more passion, gesticulating at them and repeatedly placing his hand to his ear. The crowd began clapping, sporadically at first but then in rhythm, somehow knowing exactly how to play its own important role in the spiritual bacchanal taking place on the stage.

I even found myself clapping, that is until Carlos turned and gave me a *you gotta be kidding me* kind of look.

I sighed and toned it down, but it was impossible to resist participating. The music, the crowd, the minister—it seemed to meld us all together and create a real feeling of community, as though we were a single cohesive unit, standing, clapping, and singing together. It was *fun.*

At last, after reaching its climax, everything wound down. In unison, the choir members threw their hands in the air, the music stopped, and the lights cut out. Even in the dark, I could see the crowd still standing, catching its collective breath, with some of the members dabbing handkerchiefs at their eyes. I took a deep breath, and then the lights came back on.

Rev. Clavette had used the moment to give himself a mini makeover. No longer bathed in perspiration, he was as dapper as the moment he'd entered. He allowed himself a self-satisfied smile as he gazed out on his flock, and then he began reciting one of the day's Bible readings from memory. It was a passage from Luke in which Jesus shames some of the disciples for their pretensions.

"Do you know anyone like that?" he asked. "Or maybe *you're* the one with the pretensions?" the reverend asked playfully. The crowd chuckled appreciatively.

This went on for a solid half hour, a virtuoso performance of memorized scripture followed by commentary that made you think the two-thousand-year-old texts had been written with you in mind. The Rev was impressive, and when I glanced to my side, I even caught Carlos paying attention a few times.

The service ended almost exactly an hour after it began if you didn't count the ten-minute "concert" that followed it. Almost everyone remained in the auditorium, although people were milling around and chattering. There was a distinct *buzz* in the room, almost a kind of afterglow that had people's faces blushed and smiling, even more than before the service had begun.

It would have been awkward to leave, so I stood there making funny faces at the baby in front of us, who responded by crinkling up her face into a serious frown and then bawling into her mom's shoulder. When the mom turned around, confused, I smiled and played dumb, as though I had no idea what had happened.

"First time?" I asked the woman.

She smiled. "My sister comes here, and she's been doing nothing but buzzing about this place for years, so I decided to drag Rick along and see what all the fuss was about."

Rick turned around and shook our hands. "What did you guys think?" he asked, sounding genuinely interested.

"I, well, I *liked* it," I said, trying not to gush. "I've never been to anything like this before. The hour went by like *that*."

Carlos smiled but stayed mum.

"It sure did," Rick said. "I usually hate church, but—"

"You wouldn't believe how often I hear that," a voice interrupted. Rev. Clavette had sidled up behind Rick and placed a hand on his shoulder. "Welcome, everyone!" he beamed.

I reached out to shake his hand, but he wouldn't have it. Instead, he grabbed me around the waist and pulled me close for a bear hug. "And *your* name is?" he whispered in my ear. I could feel his warmth through his suit. His cologne was understated and manly.

"Raven," I responded. He was strong, so I let the hug take its course without trying to fight it. When I'd had enough, I whispered back into his ear. "And this is my boyfriend, Carlos."

The hug dissipated swiftly as the minister eyed my beefy bouncer "boyfriend." "Very nice to meet you, Carlos," the minister lied, extending a hand.

Carlos took it. If it was possible to offer a skeptical handshake, Carlos did. The minister ignored him and turned back to me and the young couple with the baby. We chitchatted for a few minutes, and he encouraged us to stay for punch and cookies. Carlos declined, but I overruled him.

We found ourselves in a massive underground complex that looked more like an airport or shopping mall than a church basement. There were two coffee stations, a half-dozen food stands, and a giant play area for kids. Adults of all ages and colors were standing around chatting and eating as though it was perfectly normal to be hanging out in a church basement on a Saturday night.

"Look at the prices," Carlos said.

Coffee was twenty-five cents. Pizza was fifty cents a slice. "Wow. Donuts are twenty-five cents!" I exclaimed, my body succumbing to the inescapable gravitational pull of the donut stand.

"The parish must subsidize all this," Carlos muttered.

"Always about the money with you, isn't it?" I asked.

He shrugged. "It's an interesting business model. That's all."

I bought Carlos a donut, which, to my disappointment, he didn't turn down.

"Cheap junk food and an entertaining service. This is better than dinner and a movie," I said.

Carlos nodded. "Are you saying I'm a cheap date?"

"Get real," I scoffed. "This ain't no date."

Carlos frowned. "You know. You always sound like an idiot when you talk like that."

"I know," I said. "It comes from being raised by grammar Nazis. It's so unnatural for me to use anything but the Queen's English. But sometimes I do it, just to try to sound like the commoners."

He rolled his eyes as he licked the donut sugar off his fingers.

"The commoners?" he asked. "You're a damned stripper. That's pretty common if you ask me."

"Correction," I said. "I'm a stripper-slash-private-detective."

"Even lower on the totem pole," he said, shaking his head.

"Whatever." I knew he was right, so I let it drop. "Are we having pizza or what?"

He shrugged again, meaning that if we *were* having pizza, it was up to me to make it happen. Which naturally, I did.

On my way, I bumped into a few guys from the blackjack team, but neither of them had seen Dan or Laura at the service. They usually went on Sunday mornings, they explained. That's when the *real* service took place. I expressed my wonderment that anything could be a bigger production than what I'd just witnessed, but they looked at each other knowingly and smiled. "It's *big*," they said in unison.

Three bucks' worth of pizza filled us both up and then some. After a couple of free ice cream cones, we decided we'd had enough of the church for one evening and split. I knew that if I went home, I'd succumb to my donut-pizza-ice cream coma and crawl into bed, so I had Carlos drop me off directly at Cougar's where I had a few outfits I could slip into. Some coffee and loud stripper music would do the trick to keep me awake, at least long enough to make a few hundred bucks, I hoped. I wasn't sure what God would think about my going to work at a strip club directly after church, but I reasoned that since it hadn't been *my* church, it wouldn't offend Him in any way. As I've repeatedly said, I can rationalize just about *anything*.

# CHAPTER THIRTEEN

———

Sunday morning had me scratching my head. It was one of those days, increasingly common, when I woke with a hangover despite having just a single drink the night before. Or had it been three? After a few minutes, I gave up trying to reconstruct the last hour of the previous evening, knowing all too well that a fastidious and accurate recount of the previous evening's imbibing would produce a total I didn't want to admit.

Feeling old-fashioned, I took the elevator down to my lobby to pick up a newspaper and, since I was there, a couple of bear claws from the little market. Even though it was much more expensive than any other store around, I made sure to frequent the place because a couple of the guys who worked there carded me every time I bought a bottle of wine. That alone was worth the extra few bucks.

The caffeine and sugar rush that followed breakfast was as predictable as it was annoying. I wasn't a *rush* kind of person. No roller coasters for me, no skydiving, no rock climbing, and certainly no mind-altering drugs. Except for an attraction to fast cars, most of my leisure activities tended towards relaxation— spa treatments, sunsets on the balcony, and lazy, mindless novels about misunderstood loner cowboys.

I was pacing around, trying to work off the sugar energy, trying to figure out where we stood with the case of the missing blackjack money. The teams themselves had been a dead end, which Dan himself had guessed in advance. I didn't know how else to get to Laura, though. I still hadn't told Dan that I'd seen her holed up at the minister's house. After that had sunk in, I began thinking maybe I had jumped to a needlessly seedy conclusion. After all, would two people get together in the middle of the afternoon in broad daylight like that? What if one of the two thousand or so parishioners happened to drop by to seek spiritual guidance or just to drop off some nonperishable goods for the food drive? Laura had parked right in front of his house, making no secret of her presence. Wasn't it at least *possible* that their rendezvous was a perfectly innocent one?

On the other hand, she had lied to Dan about her plans for the afternoon. And, after meeting Owen Clavette, I sensed that the Reverend had a healthy type-*A* kind of sexual appetite. He'd given me an overly friendly squeeze, and he had the kind of charisma and self-possessed swagger that suggested he was a ladies' man, despite being a man of God at the same time. He wouldn't have been the first minister to tend to his flock in more than one way.

But I returned to the central problem at hand which was that any relationship that might or might not exist between Laura and Rev. Clavette didn't answer any questions about the missing money, which, after all, was the reason I'd been hired—all of which reminded me that I still hadn't reported what I'd found to Dan. I chose the easy solution. Like the coward I was, I waited until church time, when I knew his cell phone would be off. At about 9:15, I called and left a voicemail message, giving him only the basics of what I'd seen. I tried to play it down, assuring him that the meeting between Laura and Owen could have been innocent. It would be up to him to draw his own conclusions.

I had a lunch date with Alex, my recently separated banker friend. It had been my idea, but it had been hard to work up the nerve to ask him out, which made me wonder if asking someone out would *ever* be easy or if (as seemed much more likely) I would be perpetually stuck at age sixteen when it came to men. My "excuse" for taking him to lunch was the fact that he had gotten so thin and I wanted to see him eat a solid meal. To my delight, he had jumped at the opportunity.

He beat me to the restaurant and was waiting for me at the bar, nursing a tall glass of club soda. He looked better now, more relaxed. After we made our initial eye contact, for some reason, I found myself beaming at him, almost giddy. I tried to shut *that* down real fast, but there was something bursting out inside me that was genuinely happy to be there. With *him*. And I couldn't fight it.

We made small talk for a while, but lurking under the surface was something that was crying to get out, to break past the meaninglessness of the chitchat and explore the *feeling* that was going on, the passion I knew he felt for me and that I was beginning to feel for him. His eyes were burning again, boring a hole into me as I stirred my iced tea.

"Raven," he said softly.

*Buckle up,* I thought. *Here we go.* Just then, the waitress arrived to take our food orders. *Phew.* Half flustered, I ordered a burger and an order of crab cakes to share. I wasn't sure why I was getting flustered. I *liked* Alex. I knew he was a great man. Was *that* it? He was a *man*. A real live *man*. The other "men" in my life were much more like boys or, at best, adolescents. They were incomplete, hormone driven, spouting off at the mouth, impulsive, sloppy, churlish, childish, and only looking out for themselves. Alex had ten years on them, but that wasn't it. That wasn't it at all. It wasn't an age thing. It was a way of carrying himself, a mantle of quiet power he wielded through his soft confidence, easy smile, and the way his cheek muscles firmed up when he shut his jaw. This was a man of the world, a man who managed businesses and other men, who had traveled the world and had ventured something, who had taken a small bank and turned it into a billion-dollar company, and who had been rewarded for his efforts. He was scary and fascinating, and as usual, I was cautious. The fact that he liked *me* made me very nervous for some reason.

Alex was still studying the menu, caught off guard by the waitress. He settled on a grilled chicken sandwich with a salad instead of fries. Naturally. *Salad,* I thought. Well, no one was perfect.

When the waitress left us, I began babbling about my case, about the fact that I thought the minister was sleeping with my client's husband. It was a grievous breach of client confidentiality, but it was the most interesting thing in my conversational repertoire at the moment, which seemed to trump any of those concerns.

"It happens," Alex said. "These guys can exert a lot of power over people. They are role models. They're the intermediary between God and man. Some women dig that."

"And the rationalization points are right there," I piped in. "I mean, if you're sleeping with the *minister*, it can't be wrong, right?"

He chuckled.

I was fully aware that women would do stupid things for men, even for men who were losers. Rev. Clavette was no loser—he was a charismatic, handsome, powerful speaker, a guy who could get a crowd whipped up in just a few minutes. I had no doubt that if he set his mind to it, he could get a woman whipped up pretty good too. And Laura would have been a good choice, I had to admit. She was pretty, very athletic—a good catch. I wondered who else he might have thought was a good catch.

Alex was looking at me funny.

"Sorry. I was just daydreaming. I feel bad for her husband. I couldn't tell him in person, so I left him a voicemail. Is that bad?" I was suddenly feeling very guilty about how I'd handled things with Dan.

Alex cringed. "Well, it's not *good*. But there's no really good way of telling someone something like that."

He seemed to be speaking from experience. "Was your wife…?" I let the half question dangle in the air, unable to complete the thought.

He nodded. "She was projecting. She got mad at *me* for seeing you so often, but the reality is, I think she was mad at herself. She was seeing her masseuse. Nice guy, actually, gives *great* massages. But he's about twenty-eight, and I think the only thing he's after is all the money she must have promised him. I'm sure she's getting ready to clean me out in a divorce."

"She gets half," I muttered. "It's easy in Nevada."

He nodded knowingly. "Sometimes. Anyway, Raven, let's talk about something else. Why did you ask me to lunch?" he said.

The question took me by surprise. "Um, like I said, I was concerned about how skinny you were getting. You look a little better now, but the other day you looked like a skeleton! You need to eat something. And, by the way, the grilled chicken isn't going to cut it."

He waved his hand in the air and looked up at the ceiling as though my reason was so fatuous, so utterly silly, that it wasn't worthy of a response.

"Raven," he said softly, his voice gravelly again. "You expect me to believe you were concerned about my health, and that's why you invited me to lunch?"

I shrugged. Was it *that* implausible, I wondered? I decided to drop it and turn the question around on Alex. "Why do *you* think I asked you to lunch?" I asked, trying to adopt a saucy air to cover up my apprehension.

Alex chuckled. "Raven, I'm much too old for you. You know that." He didn't sound convinced, almost like he was debating the point with himself, asking for ammunition he could use on the other side of the argument, hoping I'd disagree with him vehemently.

"How old do you think I am?" I asked him.

He smiled. "Twenty-one."

I snorted up some water. "Seriously. As a factual matter, not a point of flattery."

He considered it for a few seconds, studying my face. "Thirty-two?"

"Closer," I said. "I'm older than that, but that's good enough for now. Remember, age is just a number." The last part was mostly a fib since I was dying to know *exactly* how old Alex was. I pegged him at forty-five, but that could have been a lowball estimate since he was in such great physical shape. I admitted he could have been fifty, which had a kind of psychological import for me. *Fifty.*

I was hoping he'd use the ensuing silence to volunteer his own age, but it wasn't happening. Our food soon arrived. He eyeballed my burger with what I took to be a mixture of jealousy and pity, causing me to feel the slightest twang of guilt, which I immediately brushed aside with the first whiff of the medium-rare beef combining perfectly with the dill from the pickle on top.

"Fry?" I asked, holding one out to him. I must have been a crack dealer in a previous life.

"Don't mind if I do," he said, swiping it from me and depositing it into his perfectly toothed mouth.

So there was hope, I thought.

# CHAPTER FOURTEEN

———

To my way of thinking, strippers and ministers shared one thing in common—Mondays were their quietest day of the week. The weekend was for performing, where they made their money, and the rest of the week was just prep for those few hours when they took center stage.

Apparently, I was not alone in this view. Just as I was about to bite into my first nibble of scrambled eggs, my phone rang. It was a local number, one I didn't recognize. For the first time ever, curiosity won out over hunger. I picked up.

"Raven McShane?"

"Yes," I said.

"My name is Corinne Van Fleet. I work at The Meadows Worship Center. How are you this morning?" *She was a little on the bubbly side for a Monday morning*, I thought, *but so was everyone else in that church*. I was puzzled, though, since I hadn't signed up or given them my contact info. How had they found me? I decided to play along for now and worry about that later.

"I'm very good, thanks. How can I help you?"

"Well, Rev. Clavette likes to welcome new members personally," she explained. "To get to know them just a little bit, you know, and to see how they are doing spiritually. How he can minister to their specific needs. That kind of thing."

*I'll bet he does*, I thought, keeping it to myself. I wondered if the Rev had her call every new member or just the ones with ten-thousand-dollar breasts.

"I see," I said, trying to conceal my skepticism. "So is there, like, a group orientation or something? A coffee and donut kind of thing?"

She paused for a second and then offered what I perceived was a fake little chuckle. "Oh, no. He much prefers one-on-one. Don't you? Some things are too personal to bring up in a group session. The reason I'm calling is that he actually has a three o'clock session open today due to a cancellation. Mrs. Feeney's dog needs surgery, so she couldn't make it."

*Huh*, I thought. Meeting up with a minister was about the last thing in the world I wanted to do, but if I played along, I might learn something. And Dan had paid me in advance.

"Three o'clock, huh? I suppose I could shuffle some things around," I said, trying to sound like I had something to do, which I didn't.

"Great! I'll pencil you in, and we'll see you at three." Again, too bubbly for my tastes. But, I supposed the whole church was like that.

I stared at my eggs, which were now cold and sad looking. The obvious solution was to butter up a slice of bread, add some sharp cheddar, put the eggs on top, and then microwave it for fifteen seconds to get the cheese bubbly, the butter melty, and the eggs piping hot. It was almost perfect but a little on the bland side, so I forked some horseradish onto the top, and that completed it nicely. I would have to write that one down.

Prior to my meeting with Owen Clavette, I poked around on the internet to see if it could tell me anything about him. The Meadows had a website, of course, but it was more primitive and sedate than I'd expected—certainly not the glowing, effervescent experience that the church service itself had been. All it told me was that "Rev. Owen" (as he likes to be called) was born in Illinois, had a divinity degree from Valley State Bible College (Tennessee), and had founded The Meadows Worship Center six years earlier after serving as an assistant pastor in a megachurch in San Jose, California.

*The guy moves around a lot*, I thought. Illinois to Tennessee to California to Vegas. His itinerant lifestyle aroused a bit of curiosity, so I ran his name through Google and a few other search engines. There wasn't much there apart from a few old ads for The Meadows. Most of the ads encouraged people to

visit the worship center and "discover" themselves. They would
be amazed, the ads said, about how they would "feel" afterwards.

I was no theologian, but for me, church was about
worshiping the being who created me. Whoever or whatever had
created the universe was so infinitely greater than the little worm
I was that I felt like the least I could do was give Her an hour a
week to acknowledge that fact. That's why I liked old-school
pews, the less comfortable the better, and kneelers, which were
becoming an endangered species. I wanted the Creator to know
that I wasn't above experiencing searing lower back pain from
the wooden pews, which undoubtedly were designed by some
medieval sadist, and neither did I mind getting shin splints from
the understuffed kneelers jamming into my knees. As far as I
was concerned, if you needed to see a chiropractor after
attending mass, you were in the right place. The point is, it
wasn't supposed to be about *me*. In fact, it was the one hour a
week I wasn't a self-centered little you know what. And if that
*happened* to make me feel a little bit better, then so be it. But
that was a side effect, not the purpose of going to church in the
first place.

I decided I probably wouldn't be raising these
theological issues in my tête-à-tête with the reverend. For present
purposes, if he wanted me to "discover" myself, then I would
play along and keep my mouth shut, even if keeping my yap
closed wasn't among my greatest talents. I was there to learn
about him and his relationship with Laura Hartmann, not to
debate angels on the head of a pin.

I arrived early for our three o'clock appointment. I had
dressed in a conservative blue-and-white outfit befitting the
occasion of a private meeting with a minister, something I had
never experienced. When I walked through the church office
door, the secretary I'd spoken to on the phone stood and beamed
at me for a split second, but then her expression soured almost
imperceptibly. She maintained the smile, but it was now a forced
effort rather than the genuine one she'd initially greeted me with.
There was something about me she didn't like.

I forced my own smile and sat down in an overstuffed
leather armchair which squarely faced the secretary's desk,
creating an awkward expectation that whoever was seated in the

chair would have to talk to the secretary. Luckily, Corinne had the good sense to busy herself with whatever papers she had on her desk. She wasn't selling it, though. She began frowning at a few of the papers for effect, looking oh so busy, and then she typed feverishly on the computer (still frowning) as though Western civilization itself teetered on the balance of whatever meaningless email she was sending. I kept staring at her, enjoying the show and wondering what she had been doing before I arrived. Playing solitaire? Texting her husband?

The *I'm Really Important and Busy* show ended when Rev. Owen buzzed her and told her he was ready for me. *He* was really busy and important, I gathered, too, since he couldn't even be bothered to stand up and open his own door to let me in. It was a leap, perhaps, but I was sensing a pattern of self-importance permeating throughout the little office.

"How do you take your coffee?" he asked.

"Blacker the better," I said.

He smiled and fetched me a cup, which he served on fancy china.

"Call me Owen," he said, ushering me onto a white leather couch where he joined me, crossing his legs.

I smiled back at him. *Again*, I thought, with the self-importance. The "call me Owen" thing wasn't *real*. It felt like a fake kind of modesty or folksiness that was belied by his shimmering cuff links and two-thousand-dollar suit. I called him Owen anyway. The coffee was excellent.

He asked me to tell him about myself, so I did, in a roundabout sort of way. He kept waiting for me to mention the part about how I'd been a stripper over the last decade, but I left that out of it. When I'd finished my little monologue, he remained silent, as though contemplating what I'd said.

The silence continued, at first awkward and then unbearable. It was a way of getting me to blurt something out, I figured. *Anything* to end the yawning chasm of awkwardness. I knew it was an old police trick cops employed to loosen the tongues of helpless perps, and it wasn't going to work on me. I occupied my mind by imagining what Corinne was doing outside the office. Was she eavesdropping, or had she gone back to doing her nails?

Finally, he broke the silence, and I thought I detected a pained smile creep into his expression, even if only for a second.

He cleared his throat. "Raven, er, is there anything else about you we should know? Like, for example, how do you make a living? I see from your finger you're not married, right?"

*Here it comes*, I thought. I was in a bind, though. I didn't especially want to talk about being a stripper, but I *really* didn't want to talk about being a private detective. That might have gotten his radar up, raising suspicions even though I was there at his request and even though he had no idea I was working a case that might have involved him.

I decided to come at him with both barrels. "You see these?" I asked, grabbing my breasts.

His eyebrows shot up.

"*That's* how I make a living. So you can see why I didn't mention it. It's a little embarrassing."

Owen nodded solemnly and recrossed his legs in the opposite direction. I was ninety percent sure that he already *knew* I was a stripper. After all, they'd found my unlisted phone number somehow, so it wouldn't have been too difficult, especially since I *looked* like a stripper. At least, on a good day.

"I see," he said, fumbling for words. I began to suspect I had truly taken him off guard. "Is that something you're comfortable with?"

"It pays the bills," I said nonchalantly. "And then some." I wasn't about to mention the fact that I had gotten my PI license as a way to get *out* of that business entirely.

He smiled faintly, and I could sense he was struggling to come up with an angle of approach. "Well," he began, "I'm not going to be judgmental. I don't think taking your clothes off for money is why God put you on this earth, but I also know that the records we have, including the Bible itself, suggest that many of Jesus's friends and early disciples came from the ranks of society we might look down our noses at."

"Tax collectors, prostitutes, that kind of thing?" I asked.

He nodded. "Exactly. But, Raven, we can do *better*, right? God himself wants you to flourish, to find yourself."

I shrugged, not giving anything away, slightly annoyed by the exhortation to *find myself* again. Even if I had been unmoved, a spark had been lit inside Owen. His eyes became more distant—his voice jumped half an octave. It was higher pitched but more powerful, driven by an inner spirit that had taken over the reverend's personality entirely. He began by quoting scripture, the Old Testament, and then started off on a mini homily, a personal sermon tailored just to me. Most of it was recycled material, I'm sure, but he had a way of bringing it home so that, if I hadn't known any better, I would think he had just crafted a ten-minute monologue complete with apt Biblical quotes on the spur of the moment. It was impressive stuff, I had to admit.

He continued on, sometimes appearing distant, other times looking me deeply in the eyes, holding me with a gaze so powerful I was afraid to look away. At those moments in particular, when our eyes were locked, I began feeling a kind of otherworldly, ethereal buzz that was somewhere between a caffeine high and a drunken stupor. It was a sense of utter, naked, jaw-dropped-on-the-floor curiosity about what the minister would say next about my life and my relationship with God and the universe, and at those moments, which could have been seconds or minutes or hours, nothing else mattered, nothing else could have swayed me, could have distracted me from the message that *I* was special, that *I* had meaning.

When he was done, we were both panting heavily. I was still clouded in a kind of haze, mesmerized by his performance. Impure thoughts began coursing through me. My body began craving his, I think as a means of keeping him with me for as long as possible so that I might experience that sensation again, that sense of belonging as a part of a grander plan. And partly, it was out of an insane creeping sense of jealousy, the notion that *others* would be able to share Owen's vision, that he would talk to other women in the same way. I needed to prevent that, it seemed to me at the time, and so if we got physical, I could keep him with me longer, past our allotted time. I fought a powerful urge to begin flirting with him, to give him the green light to do whatever he wanted to me because whatever he wanted was what I wanted too. He was watching me carefully, I recall, but the rest of it is fuzzy.

And that's when a danger bell began chiming deep in my subconscious. It was the warning signal that had saved me before, more times than I cared to admit. It gripped me, barely, but enough to prevent me from undressing, from giving in to the bizarre sensations that coursed through me. I remember standing up, an act that took more than one try, and stumbling out the door.

# CHAPTER FIFTEEN

———

A loud knocking sound kept penetrating my left eardrum. In my woozy dream, it was a jackhammer, a giant one, and I was astride it, for some reason believing that beneath the earth's crust lies an undiscovered river of champagne. It was just me, alone, in the desert, for some reason garbed in a baby-blue dress, confident I was about to uncover the mother lode of wine rivers, a million-gallon gusher that I could sell and drink to my heart's content. But the knocking kept coming, more insistently, and then hands were on me.

"She's breathing," I heard, rattling me out of the dream.

My eyes opened, one slit at a time.

"You okay?" a voice asked.

I wasn't okay. I felt hungover, like I'd drunk a river of champagne. And yet I knew that couldn't be true. It was light out, and my car's clock said it was just after five.

"Uh, I think I'll be okay. Just not getting enough sleep at night, I guess," I said, lamely.

The couple looked at each other skeptically. In all likelihood, they thought I was a drugged-out hooker or something. Except that I was in the driver's seat of a brand new Porsche. I looked around and didn't recognize my surroundings. It was a residential neighborhood, and I had parked the car (it was still running, I just noticed) next to, and partly on top of, the curb in front of a gray ranch house. I had no earthly reason for being there, which no doubt fueled the skepticism of the middle-aged couple who'd found me.

"Seriously, thanks for waking me up. I do this sometimes," I lied. "I was having a migraine, so I pulled over, and then it got the better of me." My voice was sounding a little less spaced-out.

"Oh, I used to get those," the woman said knowingly. "Awful things. You okay to drive home? I can call an ambulance if you want."

"No, no," I said, trying to sound reassuring. "I'm not too far. I'll be fine. It's gone now."

Their facial expressions told me they weren't quite convinced, but at the same time, neither did they want to get too involved in the health issues of a dingbat who was a complete stranger. They were more than willing to take my word for it, so I waived at them and pulled out, having no idea in the world where I was.

A block away, I pulled over, fired up the GPS, and realized I was less than a quarter mile from the church. And that's when it all came back to me, at least in bits and pieces. The reverend. His personalized sermon. The way I felt during it and after, an almost chemical kind of high. *The coffee he'd given me.* That must have been it. I remember vague snippets about how God had a plan for me—that was the main theme—but few other details. My last memory was of Owen staring at me, almost studying me, which I now realized was his attempt to see if I was going to pass out or not. I had been poisoned before and survived, so a half cup of tainted coffee wasn't going to put me under. But it *did*, I realized. It made me pass out on the road where I easily could have been killed. It was only through some miracle that I'd maintained enough sense to pull over before I clunked out.

A million thoughts raced through me. *Why did he do it? Was it just for sex?* That didn't make a lot of sense to me, although neither did half the things men did. It seemed awfully risky to drug an almost complete stranger because he'd have to expect I'd run straight to the cops. *Unless.* Unless the drug was supposed to make me *forget* everything. I wondered if that was the plan all along. I'd drink the whole cup of coffee and pass out in his office, oblivious to time and everything else, and then, once he'd had his way with me, he'd wake me up and explain that he'd hypnotized me and that everything was all right. Given his hypnotic sermons and the overwhelming charisma that made me, and presumably most other women, *want* to like him, I bet he got away with it. Maybe all the time.

My brain strained to remember any more details. Had he touched me, or did I get out of there in time? And what was Corinne doing, just outside his office? Maybe that was why she had to force a smile when I arrived—she knew what the Rev was going to do to me. It gave me the chills. I had to get past all that, though. I knew that if I wanted to bust the guy, I'd have to have my blood tested. I wasn't sure where the nearest hospital was, but my phone told me it was two miles to the northeast.

The two intake women in the ER looked at me a little funny when I told them what I wanted.

"Are you okay?" they asked in unison.

"Yes. I think so. I think I got away before anything happened."

They looked at each other. "So this isn't an emergency, it sounds like."

"But, I mean, if I'm going to file a police report, it would probably be good to have, you know, *evidence*." I tried not to sound as snippy as I felt.

One of the women rose reluctantly and went into the back where she flagged down a white-haired man with a large paunch protruding from his gray lab coat.

He nodded at the woman solemnly, checked his watch, and then told her something that seemed to satisfy her.

She returned, a petulant look on her face.

"What we'll do is this. We'll call the police on your behalf, and in the meantime, we'll run a blood test. OK?"

I shrugged. "Fine with me."

She wasn't done with me. "Most people call the police *first*, you know. So you're just a little out of order."

"Sorry," I said. "I've been drugged."

Her eyebrow shot up, but that was it. She had to admit that I had a point. "Follow me," she said curtly.

She led me into a small closet-sized room that wasn't really a room but just an area enclosed by two large blue curtains, part of a small tent city of identical quarters used for intake screenings and the kinds of tests that nurses could perform before you saw the doctor. She told me to wait and that someone would be by shortly.

Three minutes later, a rotund black man arrived garbed in salmon scrubs that matched the color of his gums when he smiled at me.

"Says here you think you were drugged," he said non-judgmentally. His name tag said his name was Winston.

I nodded. "Basically, I was with this guy, and then everything got really woozy, you know, and I got up and drove away, but I passed out and woke up by the side of the road."

He nodded, his round face a model of concern. He asked for my arm and then placed a cuff on and squeezed the little ball to make the cuff tighten. He looked off into space as he calculated my pressure through his stethoscope.

"And now the pulse," he said softly, taking my wrist. Fifteen seconds passed as I tried to lower my pulse by imagining that Winston was just about to give my arm a massage, the opening round of a two-hour full-body package at my spa.

He took his fingers off my wrist and punched something into the little computer.

"Your pulse is fine," he said. "Which is unusual."

I frowned, uncomprehending.

He leaned back in his chair. "Most people in your situation would be over a hundred just with the adrenaline flowing. You're at sixty-three which means you're still partly sedated, I think."

Then he wheeled around and rolled his chair over to a small white cabinet which held the mother lode of medical supplies and fished out a syringe. He rolled back to me, unwrapped the needle, labeled it on the side, and then showed it to me to make sure my name and date of birth were right. I nodded solemnly, and then he dipped a cotton swab in alcohol, cleaned a spot on my left arm, and smiled at me.

I'm good with needles, which has always surprised me, given my other phobias and neuroses. For some reason, I didn't mind a bit when someone plunged one into my veins. It was all over in ten seconds, but Winston didn't seem impressed at my virtuoso performance. No cringing, no wincing, no tears. I supposed most grown-ups handled it just the same.

"How long before the results come in?" I asked.

Winston smiled. "You know how that goes. Could be this afternoon still, or could be a day or two. It depends on a lot of things."

I nodded along as though I understood how things were, even though I was wondering what could be more important than a woman alleging she had been drugged.

"You're done," he said. "They told me they were calling in the police department, so you probably want to wait for them in the lobby."

I nodded and stood up. I was still hoping for a sticker, or some candy, or *something*. I left disappointed.

I returned to the lobby, surprised to see two uniforms, both female, standing near the intake desk chatting with the receptionist. In unison, they turned to look at me and then looked back at the receptionist, who nodded. They were here for me.

"We'd like to take you down to the station, ma'am," said the blonde one, a tall statue of a woman in her midthirties. She had one more chevron on her uniform than the other officer, a fuller-figured spark plug with short jet-black hair that had obviously been dyed. Neither one looked overly happy to have me on their docket that afternoon.

"It wouldn't be my first time at the station," I muttered, following them out the door.

"You got a record?" the shorter one asked. I figured she thought I was a prostitute.

"No," I said. "I'm a PI."

They both stopped hard in their tracks and wheeled around. The blonde, whose tag said her name was Fischer, gazed at me with her piercing blue eyes. "You pulling something here, ma'am?"

I shrugged innocently and reached in my purse to find a business card. I handed it over to Fischer.

"Raven McShane," Officer Fischer muttered, handing it to Officer Schwartz who looked at it and frowned.

"I've heard of you, I think," she said, looking at me funny. "You the one who proved Cody Masterson was innocent?"

I smiled and performed a small curtsy, hoping we could speed this along and get into the air-conditioned squad car.

Fisher looked at me curiously, as if the light bulb had gone off inside her head, too. "Oh, I just *knew* he wasn't guilty. He is *so* gorgeous, isn't he?" She swooned.

Schwartz, who was less impressed, rolled her eyes. "Let's get this over with," she said, cocking her head in the direction of the car.

# CHAPTER SIXTEEN

———

The officers were quiet on the drive back to the police precinct station, which was less than a mile from the hospital. Their radios blasted loud snippets of unintelligible information, which they studiously ignored, and I sat mum in the back wondering why police communication radios seemed to be stuck in the 1940s.

The officer manning the front desk nodded curtly at Officer Fischer and ignored Schwartz. He eyed me with a look somewhere between apathy and idle curiosity. They had to check me in, so I showed him my driver's license number which he wrote down with pencil on a large ledger. Again with the 1940s technology.

The two officers escorted me to a back room, which was very bright despite having no windows. Schwartz asked if I needed coffee, which I accepted, and then they both disappeared. In the ensuing boredom, I whipped out my phone and caught up on *Words with Friends* where all six of the people I was playing were beating me. *That was particularly sad*, I thought since my opponents consisted mostly of ex-strippers, cocktail waitresses, and an elderly relative I hadn't seen in fifteen years.

A new face appeared at the door, although "new" is being too kind. He was in his fifties, dressed in a hangdog, white, short-sleeved shirt with a wife-beater V-neck showing through from underneath, and his face had been through the wringer more than a few times, his nose looking like he'd gone a few rounds with Evander Holyfield. Through the gruff lines, bushy eyebrows, and hanging jowls, though, there were kindly blue-gray eyes trying to peek out. He said his name was Detective Vince Goss. It was just the two of us.

"So, you're kind of famous, you know that?" he began, a little shyly. He was stirring a little packet of sugar into his Styrofoam cup of coffee, which I guessed would be his ninth cup of the day. I thought maybe, just *maybe*, there was a hint of a blush on his face.

"That's what Officer Fischer said, but really, it was nothing," I said, referring to my first big case. Earlier that summer, I had proven that the most famous murderer in Vegas— a former star of a huge male revue show—wasn't actually a murderer at all. Instead, he proved to be a flamboyantly flaming playboy who wouldn't hurt a fly. In fact, his wife had framed *him* for the murder. The case had made all the papers and the local news, and I'd been getting business ever since.

"Nothing?" he protested. "We were all convinced he was as guilty as O.J."

"Well, the *men* were convinced of that," I corrected him. "The women, not so much."

He smiled knowingly. The common wisdom had been that Cody Masterson had been acquitted because he was simply too good-looking to imagine sending to prison.

"Anyway," he coughed. "This is serious stuff we're talking about here, Raven. Start from the beginning, if you would."

I slurped at my coffee, which I had been fully prepared to spit out in disgust. It wasn't nearly as awful as I'd imagined, so I slurped down some more, took a deep breath, and told him about the case I was working on and why I'd gone to see the Rev. Owen Clavette that afternoon. I even told him about how I thought the secretary hadn't liked me, a point he dutifully scribbled down in his report. But of course, he was most interested in how I'd felt. Had I tasted anything funny in the coffee? Was the effect immediate or delayed? What did I remember about my last few conscious minutes?

I wasn't too helpful, except for the fact that I was pretty sure Clavette hadn't actually touched me. They wouldn't be able to get him on assault charges, Goss explained, unless I remembered more than that. But they *could* get him for drugging me, which was a Class *C* felony.

"Which means what?" I asked. We had covered the various kinds of felonies in my night school PI classes, but champagne and wine had flushed all that information out of my brain long ago.

"Which means a five-year mandatory minimum but more likely ten years in the big house. And that might be just the tip of the iceberg," he said, lowering his voice a half octave.

"What do you mean?"

"I mean, in my experience, a guy like this…" He paused, taking a sip of his coffee. "This isn't gonna be the first time he's drugged somebody, if you know what I mean. He didn't just wake up one day at the age of forty, or whatever he is, and say, 'Today's the day.' This guy has done it before, I guarantee it."

I nodded. "I think you're right. I actually had the sense that the secretary might have known what was going on. Almost like she could have been the lookout, you know, to make sure no one interrupted."

He cocked his head sideways as he scratched that little tidbit down on his sheet. "Interesting theory. How long you been a PI?"

I smiled. "Couple of months. Mostly, I'm a stripper." No reason to hide it, I figured.

"I bet you make a killing," he said quietly with a bashful smile. It was a compliment.

"Pays the bills, but I'm trying to get out of it. Too many creeps."

He nodded knowingly. "No offense, ma'am, but most people in your line of work end up either strung out, broke, or dead. Not a lot of upside there. Still, there are a lot of creeps in *this* line of work, too."

*Tell me something I don't know*, I thought, but he was nice, so I kept the sentiment to myself. "Is there anything else?" I asked.

Goss made a show of examining all his paperwork and then shook his head. "Not on our end. The tox results will be back soon, and then I'll get in touch with you."

"Got it," I said, standing up. We shook hands, and he showed me out a side exit.

As I was leaving, it occurred to me that I had no car. "Actually, Detective, two officers drove me here, so…"

"Ah, yes," he said apologetically. "You're the one who went to the hospital first," he said, ushering me back inside. He left me in a hallway for a few minutes and then returned, accompanied by an officer who couldn't have been more than seventeen years old. Apparently, his rookie duties involved chauffeuring victims around town to pick up their automobiles.

He and I made small talk on the way back to the hospital, but he wasn't all that interested in my case or why I'd been at the police station. It made sense, I supposed. To me, it was a big deal to report a crime, to be a *victim*, but to him, it was just another day at the office. I thanked him and fired up the Porsche, resigned to fighting rush hour traffic to get home.

The only upside was that I didn't have to work that night. After being drugged by a creepy guy, I was in no mood to be friendly to the male sex, and so work would have been a waste of time anyway. No man would ask for lap dances from someone who was snarling at him.

After dinner, I found myself pacing nervously, checking the door repeatedly to make sure it was locked. I began wondering what I would do if I was in the reverend's position. He had half completed his crime, and now there was a half victim out there—*me*—who might turn him in to the authorities. That could make him do something crazy, something to harm me. On the other hand, I wondered if he might still be focused on completing the act he had started. Creeps like him often didn't worry so much about getting caught. They simply wanted to commit as many sordid crimes as they could. Either way, I didn't feel completely safe.

My insecurity compounded itself. As I paced around, calmed only a bit by an oversized glass of wine, I began having second thoughts about my new career choice. This wasn't the first time I had feared for my own safety, and it was getting *old*. I simply wasn't charging enough money to account for the danger, and, at that moment, I couldn't even imagine what hourly rate I'd need to charge to make it worthwhile. Danger was one of those things that didn't have a price.

Shocking as it might seem, I wasn't in the mood to drink myself into oblivion and crash on the couch in front of a bad chick movie. What I really craved was some female companionship, but I didn't exactly have a contact list bursting with options. *Chalk another one up to my job*, I thought. Detective Goss had been right—most of the girls who strip for a living end up in bad shape—and I never made any close friendships with them. Except for Rachel, my casino heiress friend, a girl I'd helped out of a big jam a few months earlier. I reasoned that being friends with one heiress was the equivalent of being friends with ten nonheiresses.

I texted Rachel but didn't hear anything back. She was AWOL. And then it hit me. If I couldn't spend time with a woman, I could call upon the next best thing—a gay man.

"Are you busy?" I asked after Cody Masterson answered on the first ring.

"Not at all. You know me. I'm like a little old grandma over here," he said, chuckling.

"Are you sober?"

He sniffed. "Define *sober*," he said.

I sighed, feigning exasperation. "So I should go over there?"

"Bring popcorn," he said excitedly.

I called down to have my car readied for me, stuffed an overnight bag full of necessities and popcorn, and headed downstairs on the elevator. The coast was clear, and so were the roads. It was only about seven thirty, but Las Vegas was *dead* on that Monday night. I arrived at Cody's McMansion within fifteen minutes.

His smile told me everything I needed to know. Cody was a "partaker," as they say, a guy who enjoyed himself a good joint every once in a while, which is to say pretty much every evening that I'd known him.

The only problem with hanging out with Cody was his looks. He was a guy who, until a few years ago, had made a living dancing around on stage for screaming, lust-addled women. And now, since he spent half of every day in the gym, I had little doubt that he could have unretired and gone back to that life. But since he had little interest in women, visiting him was a little like going to a candy store without any money.

We spent the night with some films noir, starting with *The Postman Always Rings Twice*, followed by *The Big Sleep* with Humphrey Bogart and Lauren Bacall. I never saw the end of the movie. I have vague memories of being carried up to bed, of fighting it a little bit, but when I woke up in the morning I felt more refreshed than I had in a long time. As usual, Cody had let me use his amazing king-sized bed, which was officially the most comfortable bed in the universe, while he'd slept in a guest room.

It was eleven before I finally rolled out of bed, which gave me hope that there had been word from the police about my blood test. But my phone was a blank—no calls, no messages, no emails that weren't trying to sell me something or trying to steal my personal information.

Cody was a big believer in protein, so our breakfast was a spread of sausage and eggs with some fresh melons and pineapple on the side. And coffee, *lots* of coffee. I wondered if Cody ate like this every day, and I decided the answer was yes. The man owned part of a casino and could have had a personal chef make everything, I thought. The coffee tasted like it had been brewed by his own personal barista.

"What *is* this?" I asked, holding up my coffee mug.

He flashed a knowing smile. "Hawaiian Kona. You like it? That's the real stuff, flown in every week from the islands. Not that crap they sell in the big stores."

"I'm on my third cup," I said.

After chowing down on sausage and eggs, I told him the details about the previous day, about being drugged and winding up at the police station, and when I was done, it was impossible not to smile at how cute Cody looked when he got angry. His blond hair was perfectly coiffed, and his tanned skin formed a pleasing contrast with his silky white bathrobe.

"I should go find that asshole and beat the crap out of him," he said, referring to Rev. Clavette.

"That's tempting," I said, chuckling at the image. "But the cops are handling it."

"When do you get the blood tests back?" he asked, gnawing on a pineapple slice.

"Today, hopefully," I said.

This was our fourth or fifth sleepover, I reflected, still savoring the Hawaiian Kona. We'd always done it at his place, mainly because it was so huge and because he had a movie room. And because he never seemed sober enough to drive over to my place. It was a life of pure decadence, attractive and enticing in small bits but ultimately unfulfilling. A lot like Las Vegas itself, come to think of it. The armchair psychologist in me reasoned that was why Cody resorted to smoking up most evenings. It was a conversation I would have with him at some point, but not then. I wasn't feeling preachy enough.

We parted ways with him promising not to take the law into his own hands, which aroused another few giggles on my drive home. He was certainly *strong* enough to beat the pulp out of somebody—he could crush Clavette between his abs. But he was such a playboy, a soft-hearted *bon vivant,* that the image of him pummeling someone in a fight was downright comical.

# CHAPTER SEVENTEEN

My buzzing phone jolted me out of a nap, an unplanned zonkfest that had me splayed out on my couch in a manner that pinched just about every nerve in my body. Luckily, the phone was on the coffee table next to me, so I didn't need to move much to pick it up.

It was Detective Goss.

"We've got a hit, Raven. You were right," he said.

"Huh," I muttered noncommittally. My brain was still shrouded in sleepy fog.

"You okay?" he asked. I must have sounded worse than I thought.

"Yeah, yeah," I mumbled, "I was just taking a little nap."

He chuckled. "Yeah, sure you were."

"Hey, I had kind of a rough night," I protested.

"No need to explain," he said. "I know the feeling. Anyway, I assume you're OK if we go ahead and get this thing moving, right?"

"Meaning what?" I asked, still shaking off the slumber.

"Meaning, we take this to the DA, who will begin the process of filing formal charges. Your blood tested positive for roofies, and that's pretty strong evidence."

"Yeah, let's go. I've never done anything like this before," I said.

"Most people haven't. It's not fun. I'm not gonna lie. But it's the only way we can stop guys like this. We need the victims to cooperate."

"Okay. Whatever you need me to do," I said, stifling a yawn.

After I hung up, a sense of uneasiness began spreading through my body, hitting my stomach in particular. It was reality finally hitting me, I figured. I had spent a carefree, frolicking night with Cody, and that had simply delayed the inevitable realization that what had happened to me was very serious and that it would launch a major criminal investigation. With me as the starring witness.

I could immediately see how women backed out when faced with that reality. Criminal cases took a long time, and then there would be an appeal, and in the meantime, the defendant had a hold on you, an outsized role in your life that would prevent you from ever experiencing "normal" again. But I knew what Owen had done, and I wasn't about to let him get away with it.

*Here we go,* I thought. *Welcome to your new life. Raven McShane, Victim.* It didn't have a very nice ring to it.

I realized I'd have to call Dan and tell him that the investigation was off, that as soon as this news hit the fan, everyone in the parish would know who I was. Under those circumstances, I'd never be able to uncover where the missing money went. Even so, I had a suspicion that Clavette was involved in some way. Was it being used for hush money to keep other victims quiet? There were also rumors that he wanted to build an even bigger megachurch, too, and maybe he was dipping into a number of extra sources of cash to fund that project, an undertaking that would make him an even bigger deal than he was. And those suits he wore looked like the wool was spun from the wings of angels. How did he afford all that on a pastor's salary? And what, exactly, *was* a pastor's salary?

My stomach finally settled down enough for me to make lunch, after which I did some food shopping to take my mind off things. After reading a tip in a magazine, I resolved to always do my shopping *after* a meal so as to avoid the temptations that an empty stomach makes irresistible. No chips or cookies for me, just solid foods I could multipurpose, like eggs, greens, olive oil, nuts, and cheese. We'll see how long *that* lasts.

My phone rang while I was in the checkout aisle. It was a woman named Tricia Kohlman from the Clark County District Attorney's Office. It was hard to give her my full attention since

I was busy placing my stuff on the conveyer belt and then swiping my credit card, not to mention remembering to use my grocery rewards card. But the gist of it was they wanted me to come in that afternoon to be interviewed by one of their investigators. Tricia herself would be handling the case if they filed charges. *They were moving fast,* I thought to myself. I agreed to come in. She told me I could bring a friend for support if I wanted, but I declined, chuckling at the idea. Whom was I going to bring? Carlos? Cody? Mike?

I had been to the DA's office before, just a few months earlier when I had interviewed the guy who had prosecuted Cody for murdering his brother-in-law. The guy I had talked to was a very senior prosecutor, while Tricia seemed a little bit wet behind the ears. She had me buzzed in and met me in a large open lobby on the sixth floor, a maze of cubicles and outdated computers and printer stations.

Tricia was about five eleven, sturdy, brown hair, late thirties, and sporting a complete absence of makeup. She wore an understanding smile, which must have been one of the prerequisites of her position. She was the one who had to babysit the victim, to reassure her, to cajole her cooperation, and to keep her from backing out once they had filed charges. At work, I had known gobs of women who had been abused, assaulted, and otherwise mistreated, and four times out of five, they never filed charges, preferring to stick with the devil they knew than risk being alone. It was sad, but it was one of the oldest stories around.

Tricia showed me into a small interview room with a white table and hard brown chair. I decided to clear the air right at the outset.

"Don't worry," I said, "I'm not going to back out of this."

She cocked her head slightly, taken aback.

I continued. "I imagine this is hard for most women, but not for me. I want to nail the bastard so he can't do this ever again."

It was the first time she smiled at me in any manner other than sympathetic. She was *glad.* "That's the spirit," she said, beaming. "Very refreshing."

She collected herself and then walked me through about a hundred different forms, many that required my signature. It felt like I was getting a mortgage on my house, but I just played along and scribbled my name where she told me. But after signing one form, I paused and pursed my lips.

"I don't like what this form is calling me, though," I said. "Complaining witness? It makes me sound like I'm some whiny, annoying nag."

She chuckled. "Well, technically you were just complaining about that form. So I think it's pretty accurate."

My eyes got big, and we stared at each other, trapped in the awkwardness of her joke. *She barely knows me*, I thought, *and now she's ragging on me?* And then I burst out laughing.

"I guess I can't deny *that*," I said, still chuckling. "I am, literally, a complaining witness."

Relief washed over her face. She knew she had crossed a line, but the joke was too good to pass up. *I like this chick*, I thought.

After I filled out the forms as a *complaining witness*, she had me sit down at her computer where I typed up a statement describing exactly what had happened. It wasn't the kind of story someone would fabricate, she said, and she told me the cops would canvass the neighborhood where I'd awakened to find the witnesses who found me by the side of the road.

"And what about his secretary?" I asked.

She nodded. "She will definitely play a role. My plan *A* is to get her to flip and I'll threaten her if necessary."

"With what?"

Tricia looked serious. "Accessory. She's essentially serving as the lookout, if what you're saying is true. She *had* to know what was going on in there, don't you think?"

I shrugged. "I caught a weird vibe off her right from the beginning. But I can't honestly say, one way or another."

Tricia nodded. "We'll know more once we use our leverage. A couple of burly cops and a seasoned detective sometimes make the situation a lot more real, especially if they've never had a run-in with the law before. She'll sing like a canary," she predicted.

I nodded, not sharing her rosy optimism that this was going to be easy. I knew better. She probably did, too. "Anything else from me?" I asked. I had been there almost an hour and a half by then.

She thought about it. "Nope. You're free to go. My card is stapled to the victim packet we gave you."

There was that word again. *Victim*. I think I preferred *complaining witness*. "So you'll call me when you know more?" I asked.

"Exactly," she said, standing up. "Sometimes these guys just wet their pants and blubber, spilling the beans at the first sign of flashing lights. We could get him to plead to something and be done in a month."

I felt like she was feigning optimism for my benefit, but I let it pass. I knew there was no way a guy like Owen Clavette was going to go down without a fight.

# CHAPTER EIGHTEEN

———

As had become my custom, I skipped dancing at Cougar's on Tuesday night and stayed in to hit the gym, which I had passed on earlier in the day. My gym session ran longer than usual. The treadmill had slowly melted the anxiety away in me, and then, back in my apartment, the hot tub jets worked their magic on the tenseness that had turned my shoulder muscles into taut steel cables. Despite the welcome feeling of physical exhaustion, it was a restless night, with sleep coming in fits and spurts punctuated by long intervals of *why can't I sleep?*

My client, Dan, called me the next morning, and I told him it would be a good idea to meet for lunch, if he could swing it. I met him at a little Asian restaurant near his office. An ancient Korean man was outside, working a squeegee back and forth across the restaurant's tall glass windows.

Once we ordered our noodles, he brought up what I'd told him about his wife which was simply that I'd seen her drive to the church and, in particular, to Owen Clavette's living quarters. He didn't seem too concerned about it, which surprised me.

"They have spiritual sessions sometimes," he said blandly.

"But…never mind," I muttered, cutting off my line of inquiry. If he wanted to rationalize it, that was none of my business. I had reported what I'd seen, and that was where my obligation ended. The fact that she had lied to him about her destination, and even taken evasive measures, was pretty damning in my book.

I had to tell Dan about what Owen had done to me. It would be in the news, of course, once he was arrested, but I wanted to let Dan know first.

I gave him the executive summary of what happened while he ate. Dan's head was down, his mouth slurping at a wad of noodles bunched up between his chopsticks. He looked up, chewed them, and then wiped his mouth with his napkin. He was shaking his head back and forth.

"I'm not saying that's impossible, Raven, but I really think you've got to be wrong." He said it so matter-of-factly that it made me feel like I was eight years old, like I had just suggested something to an all-knowing uncle who had shot it down as being unworthy even of discussion.

"Well, *I* was there," I said snippily. I was doing my best to avoid emotion, but Dan was being an idiot. It was one thing if he wanted to bury his head in the sand and ignore the truth about Owen and his wife, but this involved me and my own safety.

"Raven," he sighed, oblivious to the blood rushing to my face, "he's not *like* that. Sometimes people, especially women, get, you know, a little caught up in the moment. He speaks in tongues sometimes. Maybe that's what happened."

I wanted to kick him in the groin at that moment or dump scalding tea on his head, right on the spot where it was balding. Instead, I just stewed inside, raising my blood pressure and cursing the idea to go to lunch in the first place. I collected myself enough to finish off the conversation and then, hopefully, to change the subject.

"I'm not arguing this with you," I said through clenched jaws. "My purpose in bringing it up is simply a heads-up, a warning that this is coming, since I know you're tight with that whole group. I didn't want you to see it on the news first."

He shrugged. "Got it. Thanks, I guess. But I've got a warning for you then, too. A 'heads-up,' as you call it. This is going to backfire, and it's going to be painful, Raven. I'd advise dropping the whole thing altogether before you get really hurt."

I looked at him, my mouth agape and my facial expressions screaming *WTF.* I had about eight million things to say, but I simply reached into my purse, found a ten-dollar bill, and threw it on the table to pay for my half of the lunch. I scooted the chair back loudly and stood up. It was dramatic enough that the ten or twelve other people in the restaurant turned to watch, probably figuring that Dan had just dumped me or something. I sneered at Dan, turned, and stormed away from the table, feeling everyone's eyes on me. Apart from the angry click of my heels on the floor, the place had gone silent.

And then it hit me. The glass window, that is. In my pique of anger, I had been so preoccupied that I had walked straight into a wall of glass, like a bird not realizing that anything was there. Somehow, the pane had managed to withstand the full brunt of my stride, and instead of breaking, it gave a little and bounced me back, a phenomenon almost more jarring than if I had broken through. Already dazed by my conversation with Dan, I now found myself falling backwards, dropping my purse, my hands flailing out to break the inevitable collision that would come as I spun. It felt like slow motion, but I'm sure it wasn't. The air was pierced by the sounds of gasps and of chairs and tables scraping hurriedly against the floor as people dove to get out of my way. I was hitting the deck, sideways, when a table broke my fall, and I felt the sharp sting of wood on elbow, and then my wrist and hand became wet and very hot, and I knew right then that I was bleeding. *Hard.*

Half the table came down with me, including a glass of lukewarm tea that inundated my blouse. After I landed, my first concern was my arm. I pulled it up and examined it. Confusingly, there was no red liquid, no pool of blood. Instead, my wrist and hand were covered in egg foo young, someone's half eaten but still hot omelet. The hot brown sauce was still running down my arm when I noticed an unusually warm sensation coming from below which caused me to scoot to the side, only to find that I had come to rest on an entire plate of steamed dumplings, several of which were now caked on the back of my shorts. *At least they had broken the fall*, I thought. And then I thought, *there's gonna be a bruise there, a big one.* I buried my head in my chest, again feeling everyone's eyes on me, and I let out a big sigh. I wanted to cry, especially when the first snicker escaped someone's mouth, a low *pfft* of utter merriment that, no doubt, expressed the sentiments of every other diner in the place. I'm sure I looked pretty damned funny, first running into the glass window and then collapsing slapstick fashion in a tsunami of tablecloths and Americanized Chinese food. The only thing missing was the banana peel.

But I didn't cry. In fact, I started laughing. It wasn't like I *planned* it or anything, but that guy's lone chuckle had started a chain reaction in the restaurant, and I wasn't immune myself. First it was the waiter who had come over to check on me and who had appeared *very* concerned and who now was covering his mouth in a hopeless effort to stifle his laughter. And then it was the people at the table I'd ruined who began guffawing in unison, a sense of relief that I wasn't seriously hurt, which meant they, and everyone else, had the green light to laugh. Because, after all, I'm sure it had been damned funny. They had all been watching me storm out of there in a high pique and with great drama, only to strut headfirst into a wall of glass. And now I had steamed dumplings on my ass.

As I looked up, I noticed more than a few people holding their cell phones out to snap my photo, no doubt to put it on their Facebook page or tweet about it. *At least that wasn't me*, they'd write, thinking themselves very clever. The problem was that they were all laughing so hard that none of them could hold the phone still long enough to snap a good shot. A bald guy was doubled over, pounding the table with his fist, almost hyperventilating in between his high-pitched pig-like snorts. A Korean woman was leaning against the wall crying, dabbing vainly at her eyes, her mouth covered by her left hand, trying desperately to keep herself together. The laughter echoed throughout the small restaurant, building on itself, a kind of catharsis that everyone joined. The very act of everyone laughing was itself funny.

Somebody yelled out, "Do it again!" And that brought the house down all over again.

Dan was a mess, I noticed. His face was on the table, his body heaving with hysterical cackling. I shook my head. It was all his fault in the first place, and now he was enjoying it just a little too much.

I tried to take some deep breaths as I sat there on the floor dabbing a napkin on my shirt to dry it off. When the laughter had finally subsided a little, I grabbed a chair for support and stood myself up. Almost in unison, the other diners began a raucous applause, and the only thing I could do was smile and give the crowd what it wanted, which was a grandiose bow and flourish. They applauded even more, some of them standing up, even the elderly Asian man who had been washing the windows outside. I found my bag under a chair and headed for the exit, the *door* this time, but I was stopped by the guy who seemed to be in charge of the place.

*Here we go,* I thought. *He's going to stick me with a big bill for all the mess I made and the food I ruined.* But his eyes were dancing, and his face was still creased with smiles. He fished a business card out of his wallet and scribbled something on the back.

"You come back any time you hungry, lady!" he said, his English a little rough. He showed me the back of the card, which read, "25% off any meal. No weekends."

"Thank you so much," I said in mock appreciation, knowing he was trying to buy me off on the cheap. And then I got the hell out of there.

# CHAPTER NINETEEN

———

The feeling of intense, utter mortification was not unknown to me. In fact, it had become commonplace, almost an expected part of the itinerary of my life, a must-see event that played with enough regularity that I should start selling tickets. The customers at the noodle restaurant sure got their money's worth.

I shuddered and tried to shake it off. *At least I hadn't gone face-first* through *the glass,* I thought. That could have sliced my neck open, or worse. I could just picture some newspaper flunky trying to come up with the perfect headline. *Topless Dancer Now Headless, Too.*

My cell phone buzzed at me as I pulled up to the last stoplight before I got home.

"Raven, this is Detective Goss. Just a little update for you," he began.

I grunted at him.

"We went to serve the arrest warrant on Rev. Clavette. His secretary told us he was in a meeting, but something didn't feel right to our guys, so they looked around the parking lot and couldn't find his car."

"Uh huh," I said, my chest tightening ever so slightly. "And then what?"

"Well, they went back inside and confronted the secretary. Her name is, uh, let me see here—"

"Corinne," I said, interrupting.

"Yeah, yeah. So Corinne gives us the deer-in-the-headlights look, you know, 'Uh, I don't know where he is. Why are you asking?' and all that. But then our Sgt. Michaels, who's about six three and runs two fifty easily, gets close to her and starts using words like 'accessory' and 'aiding and abetting.' And she looks like she's going to break down, but…" He trailed off.

The light changed, a point I hadn't noticed until the guy behind me honked at me loudly. I zoomed through the light, crossing the Strip, and pulled into my building's valet parking lane.

"You still there, Raven?" Goss asked.

"Yup. Just parking my car," I said, still distracted. "She wasn't gonna cooperate?" I asked, trying to get Detective Goss to his point.

"Not without a little more persuasion," he said. "For now, though, Reverend Clavette is in the wind. Nobody knows where he is."

"But it's only been a few hours, right?" I asked.

"Oh, yeah. We're not too worried. He could just be at the golf course, or shopping, or whatever. He's supposed to turn himself in when he gets the message."

"From Corinne," I said.

"Yeah," he muttered. "But it's too soon to turn the screws on her. Sgt. Michaels has a feeling she's covering something up, but it's not like he's a fugitive yet, so we can't just haul her downtown. Sometimes it takes days to get a guy. Unless it's a crime in progress or a violent felony kind of thing, we don't start up the manhunt."

I sighed. There was a bad feeling developing in the pit of my stomach. A feeling I'd felt before. "Okay, Detective," I said, resignedly.

"Just don't say anything yet. I'm just giving you an update. As a courtesy. We don't want the media jumping to conclusions or scaring him off with eighteen big TV trucks outside his place. Got it?"

I nodded vigorously, even though he couldn't see me. "I got it. Just stay in touch, okay?"

"You bet," he said. "Have a good night, Raven."

"Yeah right," I muttered into a dead phone. It was two in the afternoon, I was standing outside my building watching the valet park my car, my clothes stinking of MSG and dumplings, and all I knew was that it was too hot to keep standing out there.

I took a shower and changed. The shower didn't take. Sometimes a shower could be refreshing, invigorating, even relaxing, but that one just got me wet. I made some green tea and began staring out my window, frustrated and more than a little unnerved. It wasn't just the situation with Owen. It was that this was becoming a habit—stirring up trouble and then finding myself in danger. I had just turned Owen, a very powerful man with a massive ego and a thousand or more loyal followers, into an enemy. Singlehandedly, I threatened his whole lifestyle, his little empire, his freedom. And that made me a target.

Whether the danger was real or not didn't matter. What was bugging me was that there was a legitimate *potential* for danger. This was about the fourth or fifth time in just a few months that I'd found myself with a tight chest and a rapid heartbeat, pacing around my apartment like a caged animal because I'd stuck my nose in the wrong place. I was giving up a lucrative career as a stripper for *this*? I knew I'd have to give it up eventually because my clock was ticking, and every time I turned around, there seemed to be a new girl who was barely eighteen. I *hated* them, although I knew I had once been one of them. The stripper gig would be over eventually, but did I have to quit while I was on top, while I could work thirty hours a week burning gobs of calories, all while pocketing wads of twenty-dollar bills every night?

*Yes*, I told myself. Deep inside, I knew that the same reasons I wanted to stay were the same reasons I needed to leave. As long as I was a stripper, there was zero chance I'd be able to make a normal life for myself or be able to look Fr. Sweeney in the eye while I was receiving communion. It was tempting to stick with it, to grab every last sweaty five-dollar bill, but I needed to get out. And this was the new life I'd chosen. I just had to find a way to stop ending up like *this*, fearing for my own safety and jumping at every little creak or sound.

The green tea was calming. I realized I was making too big of a deal about things. First of all, Owen might not even know the cops were coming for him. As Detective Goss had said, it was quite common that they wouldn't get their man on the first try. And even if he *did* know, why assume that he would immediately come after me? There were probably thousands of people arrested for sexual assault in Las Vegas every year, and I'd never heard of any of them trying to murder the victim after she complained. Why did I think I was so special?

I made myself a reasonably healthy dinner and vegged out on the couch, sneaking glances at the clock every three minutes. At times like that, I wanted company, to not be sitting alone in a little apartment wondering what was going on in the world outside. It was a rare moment when I *wanted* to go to work.

That Wednesday night was surprisingly busy. None of the girls knew which conventions were in town, which had me rolling my eyes and clucking like the old mother hen I was. In *my* day, we'd have spreadsheets linked directly to the Las Vegas tourism board's website, and they showed not just who was in town but *how many* people. A previous manager had even come up with a ranking system. Four dollar signs meant the conventioneers usually enjoyed our services and paid out big tips (chiropractors, finance guys, and anything related to sales or computers), while a single dollar sign (e.g., the National Accountants Board) meant "Stay at home! Don't bother with these cheapskates!"

When I got home around three, I checked online to see if there was any news about Owen's arrest, but there wasn't anything. The LVPD were known for leaking their high-profile arrests to the media, so I took it as a sign that he hadn't been arrested. I conked out on my sofa and didn't move a muscle until the sun's piercing beams began streaming through my condo just before seven, at which point, I dragged my exhausted butt to my bedroom and shut the drapes as tightly as they allowed.

My phone woke me up just after eleven. It was Dan.

"Raven, it's about Laura," he said, sounding alarmed.

"What's going on?"

"She's not at work," he said, his voice sounding rushed. "They just left a message on the machine assuming she was working from home this morning. But she left about two hours ago."

"Okay, Dan, slow down. And she's not answering her phone?" I asked.

He sighed. "No. It goes straight to voicemail. I've texted and emailed but nothing."

"Well it's only been a few hours, right?" I asked, trying to sound reassuring in spite of my growing sense of concern.

"You're right, but this is very unlike her. She never misses work. And I don't know why her phone would be off, either."

He was right, and we both knew it. "Have you called the police?" I asked.

"Not yet. I've heard they won't do anything until someone is missing for twenty-four hours, and it's only been a few," he said. "Is that true?"

"Kind of. There has to be something really crazy going on for them to get involved. And in your case, you've got a domestic situation where frankly…" I trailed off, reconsidering my reasoning in midsentence.

"Frankly what?" he asked.

"Well, I mean," I stammered, "let's just say it's a situation where the cops would not be surprised if one of you, you know, ran off."

Dan huffed. "Because of your little theory that Laura and Rev. Owen were sleeping together?" His voice was trying to mask shame with mild outrage.

"Never mind," I said. "It's not important. What's important is that we find her, wherever she is. Owen is missing, too, by the way," I blurted out.

Dan was silent now. I could imagine him trying to rationalize it, trying to cling to the last scraps of hope that his wife was faithful and that his minister wasn't a sleazebag. But Dan was a smart guy. The fact that both of them were missing at the same time was pretty alarming.

"That's not good," he whispered. "What do you mean 'missing'?"

"The cops tried to arrest him yesterday, but he wasn't there. And they haven't had any luck finding him," I said, telling him what I guessed to be the truth.

"Can they find him?" he asked.

I thought about it for a second. "I think they *can*, but I doubt they *will*."

"How come?"

"If everything I've reported is true," I began, "it's probably only an attempted assault. Even if they could prove he drugged me, they wouldn't be able to prove he planned to rape me, for example. The point is, they're not going to set up a big manhunt for a crime like that. He's a creep and a criminal, but he's not a serial killer. They just don't have the resources to hunt down every guy like that."

Dan sighed. "You're probably right. So where does that leave us?"

"Where would you run off to if you were Owen?" I asked. "Does he have a place anywhere? Family nearby?"

"Not that I know of," Dan said. "They could be anywhere," he mumbled.

*They*, I thought. He was finally admitting to himself that they were together. "I don't have any great ideas, to be honest, but I'll make a few calls and get back to you later. Let me know if you hear anything from Laura, okay?"

He agreed, and I ended the call not knowing if there was anything I could do to help him. Hunting fugitives wasn't exactly my specialty. In this day and age, if two adults with money wanted to disappear, there wasn't much to stop them.

After lunch, I decided to call Detective Goss to check in.

"Raven, I'm glad you called. I was just going to call you," he said.

*Yeah right,* I thought. "Anything happening?" I asked.

"Clavette's lawyer got in touch with us," he said. "We arranged his surrender down here at the station, and he got a quick bail hearing. So, as of about twenty minutes ago, we're done. At least for now."

"We're *done*?" I asked, surprised by everything. "What does that mean?"

"It means he's been formally charged and arrested, and now the prosecutor takes over. It's looking like a plea deal is in the works already."

I had figured as much, but it was still a little bothersome for some reason. I had been picturing him wearing orange, doing the perp walk every day as he came and left the courthouse, because the trial itself would be part of the punishment, part of the humiliation he deserved.

"Will he do time, you think?" I asked.

He paused a second before answering. "Definitely. But he's got money and a top lawyer. Between you and me, prosecutors are lazy. They roll over more for guys like that because they know what a bitch it'll be to get a conviction. So it might not be as long as you'd like."

"That sucks," I said, doing nothing to hide my frustration. "Anything else you need from me?"

"Nah," he said. "What's her name will be in touch with you, I'm sure."

"You mean Tricia? From the DA's office?"

"Yeah. That's the one. She's pretty good, I hear," he said.

After we hung up, I sighed and looked up at the ceiling. All this trouble so he can get a slap on the wrist? I supposed that's why many women didn't go through with it, especially when the assaulter was a rich or powerful guy. But, I reasoned, getting him a first offense was worthwhile. If he ever did it again, there would be no slap on the wrist. And sometimes, I knew, the publicity could bring other women out of the woodwork, women who were afraid to say anything on their own, but who drew strength in numbers. Maybe I'd be starting a wave, a wave that would crash on top of Clavette and drown him.

# CHAPTER TWENTY

———

*So Owen had gone out and gotten himself a fancy lawyer*, I thought ruefully. He was entitled, I supposed. And it wasn't exactly surprising. The kind of guy who would secretly drug a woman was not the kind of guy who would simply admit to his crimes and move on. There would be theatrics, the casting of doubt, and, worst of all, blaming the victim. I could picture it now if he went to trial. Raven McShane, the "victim." His lawyer would probably use air quotes when he said it. Raven McShane, who had done nothing with her life for the last decade except strip off her clothes and surgically enhance her body so that it was more attractive to men. More like Raven McShane, *temptress*. The more I thought about it, the more a plea deal seemed attractive.

I had a dinner date that evening with Alex, though I wasn't really in the mood. It was rare enough that I had an actual date with a man, and this was a date with a *real* man. But the situation with Clavette was weighing on me, and something else was, too. Where had Dan's wife run off to? If Clavette had turned himself in and was cooperating in the investigation, they obviously hadn't run off together as I'd suspected. The two things might have nothing whatsoever to do with each other. It was a common enough assumption, a perfectly human leap of logic to assume a causal relationship whenever *A* and *B* happened at the same time. But assumptions like that were often wrong. I had *assumed* that Dan's wife was sleeping with Clavette simply because I'd seen them together, in secret, at Clavette's home. And then I had made the leap to conclude that because both of them were unaccounted for, they must have run off *together*.

I made a little mental note to try to learn from the error, to exhort myself to not be so lazy in my mental reasoning process the next time around. And once I had done that, and once I had finished beating myself up over it, I was still faced with the question that I realized was truly nagging me—where was Dan's wife?

I assumed Dan would have called me if he had heard from her, but since it was bugging me, I decided to call him. I got no answer. It was tempting to blow it off since she'd been gone only a few hours. But with her phone turned off and with her not showing up to work, it was too strange and unsettling to ignore. All of this was weighing on me while I got ready for my date with Alex. I had insisted on a place that served real food, and so Alex had reluctantly agreed to meet me at Maria's Mexican Restaurant, which was about a mile from his office and which served an off-menu entrée that they called Mexican lasagna. It was a mixture of pork chorizo and ground beef in a heavy brown mole sauce with corn tortillas instead of lasagna noodles. It was the kind of dish that made my knees buckle. Naturally, Alex had never heard of the place.

My operating theory was that I wanted Alex to go into this relationship with his eyes wide open so that he wasn't laboring under some kind of adolescent fantasy about me. I wasn't twenty-one anymore, and he wasn't twenty-four; we were grown-ups, and neither of us was likely to change very much. So I wanted him to understand that *this* grown-up girl ate her share of cheesy Mexican food and drank more than her share of margaritas. I thought it was awesome that Alex was in such great physical shape, of course, but it was important for him to know he wasn't getting himself involved with some kind of health freak. If the expectations were lowered, gently, at the outset, then there would be no big letdown later.

*Typical me*, I thought, as I drove myself to the restaurant. Here I was, already plotting a course for the inevitable breakup, trying to make it a soft landing rather than a crash. All this before our *first* real date. Was I that much of a pessimist? I tried to think positive thoughts heading into dinner, but the disappearance of Dan's wife was still weighing on me.

Alex texted that he'd be a little late, so I jumped at the opportunity to sidle up to the bar. I hadn't been there in a couple of months, but the bartender took a look at me, smiled, and then fixed me a perfect margarita using the tequila I liked.

"Very good," I said, genuinely impressed. And then I remembered why he remembered me. It wasn't because I was beautiful or charming but because the last time I'd been there, it had been with a group of girls from the club, a going-away party for a girl who was marrying a client, a dentist from San Diego who'd taken a real shine to her. Since I had been the oldest girl and since I was the only one with more than eight bucks in my bank account, I had acted like a big shot, ordering drinks and leaving my credit card at the bar. I still remembered the exact bar tab. $482.70. It wasn't the kind of memory that would lift my spirits.

The margarita helped, though, and by the time Alex arrived, I was three-quarters of the way through it.

"You're a little overdressed," I whispered, as he joined me at the bar. He was still wearing his navy pinstriped suit, no tie.

He shrugged. "I think they'll serve me anyway. What kind of tea do they have?" He asked earnestly.

I shot him a look that was half horror and half death stare.

He smiled broadly. "Just kidding," he said, chuckling. "I'll have some single malt."

"Alex!" I hissed.

He put up his hands defensively. "Again, kidding! I'll have what you're having."

I waved the bartender over and ordered for my aristocratic date.

Alex sighed, almost imperceptibly, as he began draining his drink.

"Tough day?" I asked.

He grimaced. "Kind of. We had to let somebody go today, someone who's been with the company a long time. But I hate talking shop. What about you? You have a good day?"

I snorted up half an ounce of margarita. "Umm, no. My client's wife disappeared on us, and…" I trailed off, realizing I hadn't told him about Owen.

"And what?"

"Well," I paused. And then the margarita kicked in. On an empty stomach, it was a truth serum. "A guy tried to drug me a few days ago. And now he's been arrested."

Alex's eyes got big, and he grew very concerned as I relayed the story to him. We ordered a second round of drinks, although Alex switched from the margarita to a glass of straight tequila, and then took them to our table to order food.

Alex played along and ordered the off-menu "lasagna" with me. I realized that this was an important first date for *him* too, and he was trying to play nice and make a good impression. I had always operated under the assumption that *I* was the one being judged, evaluated, poked, and prodded, but now I understood that Alex was expecting me to be sizing him up just as much. Or even *more*.

The steaming plates of chorizo and beef arrived, and Alex did his best not to regard them with horror or even skepticism. I cocked my head at him, impressed.

"What?" he asked, gamely plunging a fork into his meal.

"I'm impressed. That's all," I said.

He put the fork down. "You know, Raven, I wasn't always like *this*," he said, waving a hand across his too-lean torso. "Check this out," he said, a mischievous smirk crossing his face. He reached down into his pants and pulled out his wallet and then handed over his driver's license.

I was still chewing my first, delicious bite, and found myself mildly annoyed by the distraction. When I'm eating, get out of my way. He'd learn, in time. I examined the driver's license, front and back.

"What am I supposed to be looking at?" I asked.

"Look at the picture."

"Uh huh. *And*?"

He sighed. "I used to be fat," he said, taking the ID back.

I looked at it again and then checked the weight listed on the card. "Ooh," I said, mockingly, "you were a hundred and eighty-two pounds. A real chunker."

He shrugged.

"That's still thin," I said. "Most men are, what, two hundred? According to experts, whoever *they* are, two-thirds of the country is overweight." I bit into another delicious bite of cheese and meat, the irony not lost on me.

I was waiting for Alex to take a bite, and when he finally did, he pronounced the food delicious and dutifully began to finish his plate, just like a good boy. And then my phone buzzed. It was a number I didn't recognize and, despite being on a date, I answered.

"This is Owen," the voice said. "Owen Clavette. How are you, Raven?"

His voice gave me chills, a flashback to our last encounter. I tried to collect myself enough to respond, although part of my brain was telling me to just hang up.

"You shouldn't be contacting me," I said. "You've got a criminal case going on, don't you?"

"For now," he said, a little too casually. "I was hoping we could get past all that."

Alex must have read my body language because he piped in. "What's going on?" he whispered.

I held up a finger to Alex to signal that I'd tell him in a minute. I needed to focus.

"What are you suggesting, Owen?" I asked. In the back of my mind, I knew there might be some way out of this, some way for him to walk, and I wondered if this was it.

"I'm suggesting we meet and just talk," he said. It sounded rehearsed. "I think there was really a big misunderstanding, which was entirely my fault. And there would, of course, be some…recompense, to accommodate you for the inconvenience of everything."

*Recompense*, I thought. What a word. More like *bribery*. Still, I wasn't completely above being bribed. "And where would this meeting take place? I'm not going back to your place," I said firmly.

"No, no, of course not," he chuckled, trying to sound like the friendliest sex predator in the world. "It can be anywhere you want. Somewhere right out in public, if that would make you more comfortable."

"It would," I confirmed. No doubt about that. My mind was racing, trying to think of a good spot. And then it hit me. It was so obvious that it had taken a minute. "Let's meet at Maria's Mexican Restaurant. A mile north of the Strip, off of—"

"I know where it is," he said, cutting me off. "They have great margaritas there."

I cringed at his tone of voice. Owen was trying to be so conversational and friendly, as though nothing had happened. It was insulting.

"When can you get there?" I asked.

"Twenty minutes."

"Do it," I said and hung up. I looked around me, surveying the room. Ten or twelve people dining in the restaurant plus a half dozen at the bar. Safe enough, I decided. If Owen wanted to try anything with me, he'd have a hell of a time.

# CHAPTER TWENTY-ONE

———

Alex was frowning at me, his face a mixture of puzzlement and concern. "Sorry," he said. "It was impossible not to overhear a lot of that." I noticed he'd stopped eating.

"Finish your plate," I instructed only half jokingly.

"Yessum," he said with a deep Southern drawl and a wide smile.

I moved my half-finished margarita to the empty table next to us to prevent me from instinctively slurping it down. I wanted whatever wits I had to be fully engaged by the time Owen arrived. Since I hung up, I'd been getting a bad feeling about the meeting.

"You want to stick around?" I asked Alex, trying to make it sound like a casual inquiry rather than the desperate entreaty it was.

"Wouldn't miss it," he said, dabbing a napkin at his mouth. "This stuff really is pretty good, I have to admit." He surveyed his nearly empty plate. "Did I eat enough to get dessert?"

I shook my head. I guessed I had it coming, acting like a schoolmarm and ordering him around. "Let's wait on dessert," I said.

Alex pretended to look injured and then leaned back in his seat. "All right, now are you going to tell me what's going on or not?"

I nodded. "You want the short version?"

"No."

"I was afraid of that," I said, checking my watch. We still had fifteen minutes, so I filled Alex in on what I'd been up to, starting with the card counters who were missing money, the disappearance of my client's wife, and then the business with the preacher who'd drugged me.

"And he's coming here in five minutes?" Alex asked, incredulous. "I'm no lawyer, Raven, but I think that's against the law. He can't just call up a witness in a criminal case and say, 'Hey, let's chat!'"

I smiled. "You'd be surprised at what people do. You're working at thirty-five thousand feet up there in the clouds in the boardrooms of the business world. Down here, people are scrappers. This guy does *not* want to lose what he's got, so he's going to try to buy his way out of it."

"And you're going to let him?"

"No," I said. "Well, *probably* not. We all have a price." I didn't believe Owen had enough money to meet *my* price, whatever it was, but I was just being honest.

"We've got to get this asshole off the streets," he said.

"I know," I said. Alex's anger was palpable. I decided it was better if he wasn't privy to my conversation with Owen since I didn't feel like breaking up a fight at the moment.

"He should be here soon," I said, standing up. "Let's go to the bar and wait."

Alex joined me, and I politely suggested he sit a few stools down from me, as though we weren't together.

"Keep checking your watch," I said. "That way, he'll think you're waiting for someone."

Alex was about to say something, but then he bit his lip. "You're the boss," he said.

*Wow*, I thought. Alex was handsome, rich, and *trainable*. The trifecta of potential boyfriends.

We spent the next five minutes pretending not to know each other, not that it would have mattered much. Although I was happy to have Alex there for moral support, it wasn't like Owen could try anything when there were dozens of people in the restaurant.

I ordered myself another drink, out of pure habit. After all, I was sitting at a bar. I was stirring the margarita aimlessly when I sensed a presence behind me. The presence cleared its throat.

"Raven," he said.

I spun around on the bar stool, not standing up. Owen was dressed in a crisp blue golf shirt tucked into khaki pants with a dark-brown belt. He wore an ambiguous smile on his face as he greeted me, which gave me the chills. I felt like I was talking to a mannequin at Macy's.

"Let's make this quick," I said. "You shouldn't even be here."

"May I?" he asked, gesturing to the stool on my left.

"It's a free country."

He sat down and waved away the bartender. I figured Owen wasn't much of a drinker. He got off on power and fame, not booze.

"Like I said on the phone," he began, "I think there's been a big misunderstanding here. I mean, consider this from my angle for a minute. Imagine how the church is going to feel when their leader gets dragged through the mud like this. Imagine the effect on the children, who look up to me, and their parents, who rely on me for comfort and hope, a beacon of the Lord's message that they can—"

I cut off his bullshit machine. "Cut to the chase, *Reverend*," I said. I wanted to slug him, but that probably wouldn't look good to a jury.

"Okay, okay," he said, again with that plastered-on mannequin smile. "To make up for any confusion and hardship you might have thought you experienced—and we would have to sign something agreeing that this was just a misunderstanding—I would be able to offer you—" Owen's offer was cut short for the simple reason that a beer bottle had been smashed over his head.

I hadn't noticed, but Alex had gotten up from his seat and had been eavesdropping on our little conversation. Apparently, it had been too much to take, and he'd borrowed some poor guy's Dos Equis, which, as luck would have it, was more than half full, judging from how wet Owen's head was.

Owen spun around, completely dumfounded. Alex's anger was bubbling over. He was breathing deeply and had a look of pure malevolence on his face.

"Get out of here, you piece of shit," he said, his voice low and commanding.

Owen had blood and beer dripping down from his left ear but otherwise seemed well enough. He muttered something incomprehensible and then came to his senses. "And who the hell are you?" he asked, finally.

"Doesn't matter who *I* am. *I* know what *you* did, and it makes me sick that people like you are allowed to roam free. I repeat, get out of here." Alex pointed at the door for effect. The bartender had been mopping beer off the bar and had discreetly picked up the phone, probably to call the police in case things got out of hand.

The manager finally arrived, flanked by two stout Mexican busboys. Both Alex and Owen looked at them and then at each other.

"He was just leaving," Alex said, motioning to Owen.

Owen straightened himself up, sensing he had lost the room, and walked towards the door, grabbing a napkin on the way out and holding it up to his head.

The manager flashed a questioning look at Alex as if to say "What the hell was all that?"

"The guy's a criminal," Alex said vaguely, "in violation of a restraining order." That seemed to mollify the manager who turned his attention to Owen who had hurried his pace to get to the exit.

Alex looked at me. "Sorry," he muttered. "But that guy is scum. I could just tell."

I shrugged. Half of me was pissed because I didn't get a chance to hear Owen's offer. But half of me was experiencing a bit of thrill, a medieval tingling over the fact that I had aroused so much passion and anger and that grown men were fighting over me.

Alex looked around the room, aware now that he had become the center of attention. It was a completely incongruous scene. There was Alex, dressed like the banking millionaire he was, breathing heavily and still looking slightly crazed. Beer had sprayed everywhere. Instinctively, Alex reached in his wallet and found a crisp Benjamin. He found a dry spot on the bar and then slid it across towards the bartender. The bartender nodded curtly, Alex's offense instantly forgiven.

"I think we should get out of here," I whispered.

"Don't you want to finish your drink?" he asked. He was probably joking, but he didn't know me very well.

I pulled out the straw, tipped the glass back, and drained the rest of the margarita. After I licked the salt off my upper lip, I calmly placed the glass back on the bar. "Ready," I announced.

Alex and I made our way to the door, ignoring the curious stares of the other patrons.

"This is my second dramatic restaurant exit of the week," I muttered.

He shot me a look.

"I'll explain later," I whispered.

When we got to the door, I pulled Alex back.

"Check that out," I said, pointing discreetly at a black Lexus in the parking lot. Owen was bent over, leaning down to talk to the driver.

"I wonder who that is," Alex said, just loud enough to penetrate the piped-in Mexican trumpet music.

We watched, keeping our distance. Owen kept looking back at the door, as though expecting us at any minute.

"There has to be a back exit," I said, eyeing the car. "I don't like the way this looks," I whispered. I couldn't see the driver Owen was talking to, but the fact that he had backup was disturbing.

Alex nodded. "You thinking he's here for you?"

I shrugged. "Could be," I said. "If you stood a lot to lose based on a single witness' testimony, wouldn't you think about bumping off that witness?"

This last part must have been overheard by a passing waitress because she turned around and gave me a puzzled look. I glared at her, and she quickly retreated, probably deciding she'd heard me wrong.

"They're not expecting *me*, though," Alex said. "I'll pull my car around back and meet you there."

I nodded. It probably was an overreaction, but I didn't feel like exposing myself at the moment. "What do we do about my car?"

"I'll have someone get it back to your place," Alex said.

"If you say so. Let's go."

I watched Alex get to his car without incident, and then I weaved my way back through the restaurant. There were no other public exits, but that only meant I'd be taking an unscheduled trip through the kitchen. I spotted the double doors and followed right behind a teenage boy who was carrying an empty tray. The red *EXIT* sign glowed in the far corner of the kitchen, which was a cacophony of chopping, sizzling, and ordering given in rapid-fire Spanish. I smiled at two of the cooks who looked up from their work, but apart from them, no one paid me any attention.

Alex's Mercedes-Benz was idling right outside. I double-checked to make sure no one was watching, and then I slipped in.

He handed me a golf hat, which I reluctantly donned, and then I slipped down in the seat while we exited the lot.

"I don't think they noticed," he said.

We pulled up to a red light. "Now what?" I asked.

"I was just thinking that. You probably don't want to head right home, do you? I mean, with that scary-looking guy…" Alex trailed off and then cursed under his breath.

"What?" I asked.

"There's a black Lexus a few cars behind us," he said.

"There's probably five thousand of them in this town," I said.

"Still."

The light changed, and we drove ahead, slower than at normal speed. I wasn't sure if Alex was just an old-man driver or whether he was trying to let the Lexus catch up. I couldn't see much in my rearview mirror.

Alex was obsessively checking his own mirror.

"Don't keep checking, or he'll notice," I said. "It's called information asymmetry." I pulled that term out of left field, but it fit.

Alex snorted. "You sound like one of my consultants."

"The point is, *if* we're being watched, we don't want the watcher to know that we know. That gives us an advantage." It sounded like a real-life private detective thing, but really it was an idea I'd borrowed from the world of poker.

"You're the boss," he said.

As best as I could tell, the black Lexus was still trailing us by two car lengths. Since we were doing five miles under the speed limit, that was a little strange.

"Most cars would have passed us by now," I said. "But he's staying back there."

"Screw it," Alex said. "I think we have to assume it's the same guy and that he's dangerous. That means you'll be my guest tonight."

I cocked my head to the side. "What's one thing got to do with the other?"

He turned and flashed me a thin smile. "I live in a gated community," he said. "I'll phone ahead."

He punched the car's touch screen a few times and found the number for the front gate.

"This is Alex McConnell," he said. "I'll be at the gate in about five minutes. There is a black Lexus behind me that I do *not* want admitted. Got it?"

"Yes, sir," said the voice, and then Alex hung up.

"You ever have a first date like this?" I asked.

"This is nothing," he said jokingly. "I once dated a Russian assassin. And then there was the Ukrainian spy. Svetlana was her name."

I chuckled, grateful for a little comic relief. We were entering a more exclusive part of town now, where the streets were named with whimsical Anglo references like Avalon Lane, Meadowshire Court, and Windsor Drive.

The Lexus was still behind us.

Alex pulled into a well-maintained long driveway lined by ubiquitous palm trees. We curved around a bend, where the security gate appeared. Actually, it was more of a security *house*, a small red-brick structure with a large window revealing not one but two guards sitting inside. A sign warned *No Admittance Without Identification.*

"He's still back there," Alex said.

I checked my mirror. Too late, the driver had realized he was heading up a dead end. Either he was going to have to back out awkwardly or do a U-turn at the security gate. Or he could take the guard by storm in a firefight, and then we'd all go down in a hail of gunfire.

The security guard smiled at Alex and then pointed at the Lexus behind us.

"That the car you called about, sir?" he asked.

Alex hushed him. "Just pretend it's not there, unless of course he tries to get in. We don't exactly want him to know that we know he's following us."

The guard seemed to take a few seconds to comprehend, and then he smiled. "Got it, sir. We won't let him by."

Alex nodded and then eased his car through the security gate, which the guard had opened. When I checked my mirror again, the Lexus had disappeared.

"He's not following," I said.

"That's probably a good thing. I don't think Leon there would have put up too much of a fight."

I was barely paying attention to Alex. Instead, my attention was dominated by the mansions we were passing, many of which had to be north of ten thousand square feet. Unlike many Las Vegas neighborhoods I'd been to, however, these homes all looked classy and stately rather than obnoxious. The neighborhood fit Alex nicely, I decided.

He weaved the car into a cul-de-sac and then pulled into a long driveway that led up a steep hillock and then swerved around to the left where his house lay in front of us. After seeing all the mansions on the way in, I couldn't avoid a small pang of disappointment upon seeing Alex's house. It looked like a mission-style ranch, the kind you might see in California, with clean lines at right angles and no ornamentation whatsoever. It was big and beautiful and in great taste, but it was no mansion. Alex pulled the car into the four-car garage and then, after parking, he raced around the front of the car to open my door for me. I took his hand and smiled at his gallantry.

"Nobody saw us come in, right?" he asked.

"Not that I could tell. Why?"

"Just paranoid about my wife, is all. She's probably gathering dirt on me to use against me in the divorce. If they get some snapshots of me bringing a…" he trailed off.

"Bringing a *stripper* back to your house?" I asked, following him into the house.

"Well, yes," he said, a little embarrassed. "That's it exactly. Come on in," he said. "I'll show you the guest rooms."

*Rooms, plural*, I thought. Interesting.

I followed Alex down a hallway, and within five seconds, I realized I had been wrong. Very wrong.

The hallway was elevated, with hardwood floors suspended by steel cables, our path glassed in up to waist level. It turned out we had entered on the third floor of the house, and I now found myself looking down at a massive three-story atrium, a monument to modern architecture—glass and steel everywhere, with the same wood floors on each level. This was no humble ranch house. It was a megamansion.

"This is beautiful, Alex. It's a little deceiving from the front," I said.

He smiled. I'm sure he'd heard the same comment a hundred times. It turned out that the house had been built into a hill that concealed the bottom two floors in front. But from my vantage point, I could see down into the kitchen and through its floor-to-ceiling windows out into the backyard where there was some kind of party deck and a giant pool.

I wasn't done taking in the view, but he rushed me along the hallway and to a corner suite which looked out over the backyard.

"This is the *guest* suite?" I asked. "I can't imagine what the master looks like."

The room, although heavily modern, had rough stone inlaid into the walls which gave it a warm feeling. The bathroom had slate-gray floors and a giant soaking tub, and there was even a little nook around the corner that had a marble countertop, sink, and microwave, and the all-important coffee maker. There was even a little basket of different kinds of coffees.

"This is like being at the Ritz," I muttered.

"It's nice enough," Alex said, a little embarrassed. "Now, Jeeves will be along in a minute to get you settled in and fix you some tea."

He said it so seriously that I fixed him with a confused stare.

Alex smiled. "Just kidding. There's no Jeeves. You want a snack? I'll whip something up." His voice had raised a half octave.

He was a little nervous, I realized. It dawned on me that this was probably the pinnacle of his fantasy. The stripper girl he'd been lusting after for years was now inside his own home, his wife was out of the picture, and he wasn't sure what to do. Like all men, he was a bundle of hormones, but his were tamed by his impeccable manners and Tennessee charm. All in all, his nervousness was irresistibly cute.

I followed him down two flights of stairs, marveling the whole time at his house, which had the feel of a medium-sized office building except that it managed to be warm and cozy, despite its size. The floor where I would stay had two other guest suites, he said, plus a workout room. The second floor had the master suite, which he skipped on the tour, and a library that looked like it had ten thousand books in it.

"Ever heard of Kindle?" I asked. "You could put all of those on one little device."

He frowned. I had disappointed him somehow, but he was trying to get past it. "You *could*. You could put all of Mozart's symphonies on a little iPod, too. But—"

I couldn't help cutting him off. "It's better to have the vinyl," I said, completing his thought.

He smiled, indicating I was forgiven. "What a view," I muttered, looking out over the backyard. Most of the yard was covered in the typical Nevada gravel, a colorless dun-brown feature that I found a poor substitute for good old-fashioned grass. But there was a manicured path through sculpted shrubs and trees, a sitting area around a gazebo, and a pool area that would have looked right at home at a Ritz-Carlton on the French Riviera. Not that I'd ever been *there*.

We proceeded downstairs and into the massive chef's kitchen, a study in steel and stone, with white cabinets adorned with sleek black hardware. Alex was fumbling around in the fridge, probably because he was unprepared for a visitor.

I wasn't especially hungry, having eaten like a prized pig at Maria's, but it gave Alex something to do while I adjusted to his home. He ended up finding some fresh mozzarella and began slicing it into little cubes, and then he grabbed a tomato and cut that into similarly sized bites. A dash of basil, some salt, and a healthy glug of olive oil went into a bowl, and he mixed it all together. He disappeared into the pantry and returned with a pint of almond gelato and little Italian cookies.

"Just dip the cookies in there," he said. "It's best if you wait a minute until it melts a little."

I snorted in spite of myself. There was no way I'd be waiting until the gelato melted. It was delicious, if not messy, and my stomach accommodated it by making some extra room.

After a minute, he bent down to a hidden refrigerator and pulled out a bottle of white wine. The label was French, but apart from that, I couldn't tell what kind it was. Not that it mattered. I was thirsty.

"This is amazing," I said, the chalky and crisp flavor still lingering in my mouth long after I'd taken a sip.

He smiled, a little embarrassed again. He hadn't prepared for company, and I wondered if he might be a little bit uncomfortable letting a stranger see how lavishly he lived. Inevitably, I moved towards the windows and the door that opened up into the backyard.

"There's a great shady spot out there," he said. "I'll show you."

He poured himself a glass and grabbed the bowl of Italian salad. I followed him into the back, which at first was a maze of carefully sculpted greenery and then turned into an expanse of marble and shimmering blue water. There was almost no ornamentation, in keeping with the style of the house. Just rectangles and squares, the clean lines allowing the symmetry of the design and the ubiquitous marble to express an effect that was as calming as it was classy.

It was twilight now, and the pool was lit from underneath, while an endless parade of LED lights was lined up around the paths and the shrubs, sunken into the ground. It was breathtaking. I had rich friends like Cody, and I'd been to the homes and apartments of wealthy clients, but I'd never seen anything like this. It was, above all else, a study in perfect taste.

We sat down in some lounge chairs to enjoy the dusk, the temperature cooling down into the seventies in anticipation of its plummet to the fifties at night. Alex admitted that he'd been a "part" of the home's design team, which I took as a modest admission that he'd done most of it by himself. The crass American in me was trying to calculate the cost. Was this a five-million-dollar place, I wondered, or was it even more?

"I hate to ruin the mood," Alex began, "but you don't seem too freaked out that we were followed here."

I smiled. "I've been followed by Russian spies and Ukrainian assassins," I said, recalling his earlier attempt at humor. "A guy in a Lexus is nothing."

The truth was, Alex was right. I admitted to myself that a significant part of my brain, the womanly part, had been jumping the gun, picturing myself living in this house, living with Alex, starting a new life without creepy guys ogling and pawing at me or bad guys chasing me. It was pure fantasy, I knew, but it had clouded my senses, pushing back into my mind's recesses any notion that I should be afraid right now, that a guy had somehow managed to follow me even after we'd taken evasive measures at the restaurant.

He shrugged but didn't drop it. "They'd have no way to know which house I lived in, right? I mean, there are twenty-four homes in this subdivision, all behind the gates."

I nodded. Sometimes you believe what you *want* to be true rather than what was actually true. This was one of those times. "If they were industrious and motivated," I said, "they could have your plates run and get your address that way."

Alex cringed. I sensed he was reconsidering his decision to offer me shelter, or at least to get involved with a nut case hot potato like me. He got up to fetch the bottle of wine from the kitchen. I found myself staring out at the expanse of the backyard, wishing that the lights by the pool weren't so bright because they made it seem like something was moving out there between a couple of trees far down the hill.

By the time Alex returned, I had decided that I would not be sleeping with him that night. Part of me wanted to, of course. He was very likely the best man I'd ever met, and I was willingly letting myself get swept up into his fairytale of a life. And I knew that, with someone chasing me, I'd sleep better in his room, next to his strong, protective body. But my womanly sense told me that, if this was going to work in the long term, I had to hold off, to deny ourselves what we both wanted. To play it slower.

We enjoyed a partial view of the sunset with its purples and reds gradually morphing into a color wheel of pastels. Almost imperceptibly, nature's soundtrack changed from dusk to evening, with the occasional whirr of a bat's wings and the unmistakable call of desert owls screeching from their unseen perches.

"You mentioned Mozart before," I said, interrupting our silent enjoyment of the dimming sky.

Alex smiled. "I didn't like him when I was younger. That *Amadeus* movie made him out to be a real jerk, a kind of playboy with more talent than art."

"But now? A change of heart?" I asked.

"Part of it was a trip to Austria I made a few years ago. The man's a national hero over there, and it got me to take a second listen. I put him up there with Brahms, Beethoven, those guys." He took a sip of his drink. "Not that anyone cares what *I* think," he added, chuckling.

"I'm more of a Wagner girl," I said. "I like it loud and bombastic, over the top."

He turned to look at me, and I thought he looked impressed. He probably wasn't expecting his stripper fantasy to have an opinion about classical music.

"Wagner," he muttered. "He was another jerk. But some of those operas are fantastic, I'll grant you that."

We batted names around, back and forth, names I had learned from my grandma's collection of old records, recordings from the famous conductors in the fifties and sixties, the heyday of symphony orchestras when even cities like Cleveland and Milwaukee were putting out world class performances. Before we knew it, the sky had become pitch-black.

# CHAPTER TWENTY-TWO

———

"We better get inside," Alex said. "It's getting cold out here."

He wasn't kidding. The wine had given me the false sense of warmth, but I had found myself shivering every couple of seconds against the plummeting temperatures.

*Now for the awkward part,* I thought. Being the gentlemen he was, he would make a demonstration of showing me to my own room complete with en suite facilities and on a different floor, with its own set of linens and towels, and probably even a toothbrush. All the while, he'd be hoping that I would decline the offer and try to seduce him, or at the very least, I would sneak into his bedroom when the lights had gone down.

It was close to nine thirty. Too early to go to bed. Alex took me into a studio on the first floor, a large windowless room with acoustic lining on the walls and speakers coming out of the ceiling. He led me into a gigantic closet which proved to be a musical library, almost all of which was vinyl. He found a shelf marked *W* and drew a plastic-covered sleeve out, turned it over in his hands, and then handed it to me.

"Wow," I muttered. It was a recording of Georg Solti conducting the Vienna Philharmonic in *Das Rheingold* from 1958, a recording I recognized as a classic even though I'd never actually heard it.

Alex took it back, disappeared into another smaller closet, and then escorted me out of the library and back into the studio. He directed me to a comfortable recliner and adjusted a pair of headphones to fit my head.

"May I?" he asked.

"You may," I said, giggling as he gently placed the headphones over my ears.

I heard the telltale scratching of a needle on the vinyl record, although it was so muted that I soon forgot it was there.

And then it started, the familiar low cry of horns followed by other horns, probably French horns and trombones, joining in with a study in smooth harmony in a major chord. The strings then started up, violins, violas, cellos, layering on top of the harmony. I found myself lost in it, my eyes closed, and when Alex touched my shoulder, it was like awakening from an Alpine dream. He was smiling.

"That sound quality is amazing," I said. "It's like being there live."

He was beaming at me. "My wife hates all this stuff," he muttered. "She thinks it's a waste of money." She'd say, "Who would ever just sit in a chair and listen to music?"

"I do it all the time," I said. "I might never leave if I had a room like this!"

Alex looked as excited as a kid on Christmas morning, I noticed, so I decided to tone it down a bit. As with other men, my fear was that his infatuation, which was based on sexual attraction and a single shared interest, would fizzle out and be replaced not by a deeper, more meaningful relationship but by nothingness and boredom. I was never sure if my strategy was right—after all, I was still *very* single—but it was the one I was going with.

I let out a yawn, recalling that the queen-size bed in the guest room had looked plush and inviting. It was almost eleven, a reasonable bedtime for anyone, especially Alex who I assumed had to work the next morning.

"Getting late," I said.

Alex kept a poker face, pretending not to be disappointed. "Yes, of course," he said, as though he was about to make the same observation himself, which he wasn't. "Let's go upstairs."

He led me up the stairs, although I assumed there was an elevator somewhere, and both of us found ourselves catching our breaths after two flights of stairs.

"Here you are," he said, giving away nothing.

"Amazing house," I said, and leaned in to give him a peck on the cheek. "A date to remember, for sure."

He smiled. I thought I detected a hint of disappointment in his face, but he was too kind to let much show through. And he certainly wasn't going to beg for it. "If you need anything, you know where I'll be," he said ambiguously. *At least he had a sense of humor*, I thought as I closed the door.

I knew it must be killing him, but I wasn't going to budge. He would probably thank me later, I reasoned. *No*, I thought. *That was thinking like a girl.* Men just wanted it, and they'd never thank you for not having sex with them. That was not part of their vocabulary.

The room was the perfect temperature, and the bed was indeed plush, with ample covers and a dark-red duvet in case it really got cold during the night. Without any other options, I decided to sleep in my clothes.

I had never been good sleeping in strange beds, but there was something about this one that made me feel safe and at home. I had forgotten about my worries, at least temporarily, although nighttime is when they have a way of bubbling up to the surface, getting in the way of sleep. But somehow my natural grogginess won out, and I managed to doze off within a few minutes of hitting the pillow.

I was in the middle of a bizarre dream where I kept getting ice cream sundaes dumped on me when I heard it. It wasn't one of those sounds that you hear off in the distance, slowly arousing you out of your slumber. It was more like an air raid siren, a blaring and obnoxious assault on the senses. All the lights had come on. There was a loud knocking on my door, and then Alex entered, all before I could figure out what was happening.

"Let's get down to the basement," he said. "Just leave everything here."

I had no argument to the contrary, so I followed him down the stairs, taking them two at a time, trying to shake myself out of the peaceful sleep I'd just been enjoying.

We passed through the first level, near the music studio, and then Alex opened up a hidden door which led to another staircase. He showed me through and then closed the door behind us, locking it with a deadbolt.

"Turn right," he said, using a loud whisper. The basement was finished but unfurnished, and it was dimly lit.

"In here?" I asked.

He nodded. "That's the safe room. Quickly." He pressed his hand on the small of my back to usher me in, and then he swung the large steel door shut behind us. It made a whooshing sound as it closed, suggesting a hermetic seal.

It wasn't much to look at from the inside. There was a communications box with a little laptop computer attached to it and no windows. It felt like being inside a bank vault.

"Okay," he said, speaking to no one in particular. "If the alarm went off, it means someone was outside."

"Ever have a false alarm?" I asked.

"Actually, it's never gone off before at all," he said. He was still panting a little bit from our mad scurry downstairs. "This is the first time since we had it installed, about five years ago now. But it's set to detect human activity, not owls or coyotes. I would trust it, especially under the circumstances." *He wasn't dressed like a multimillionaire*, I thought to myself. A white T-shirt on top of some beige silk boxer shorts showing off toned legs with a little black hair on them. "So, what now?" I asked, my eyes still on his bare legs.

"Well, supposedly the police have already been called by the system," he said.

"But they won't know what the situation is unless we tell them first," I said. "The computer won't know anything apart from the fact that human movement was detected. What time is it, anyway?" I asked.

He hunched over the computer and squinted hard. "Looks like one thirty-eight to me," he said. Apparently, Alex was a wearer of contact lenses, which he would have removed before going to bed.

I pulled out my phone and checked it. As I'd suspected, there was no service down here.

"Does that phone work?" I asked, nodding at the phone on the wall.

"It should," he said. "I pay the bill every month."

Sure enough, there was a dial tone. My first call was to 9-1-1 where I filled in the dispatcher. She was interested to know that we were in a panic room, which was something she had never dealt with. Only rich and famous people had panic rooms in their homes, I figured, and they didn't call 9-1-1 very often.

My second call was to Carlos. He'd still be working at Cougar's at that hour, and the club was loud, but I knew his phone was always set on vibrate. I explained the situation to him, and he eagerly agreed to drop everything and drive over. Just like the dispatcher, he had seemed interested in the panic room.

"A damsel in distress," he mused.

"Just get your ass over here," I said, shaking my head.

"Who was that?" Alex asked.

"A friend of mine. You might recognize him. He's a bouncer at the club who sometimes helps me out. And he's got three or four guns," I added.

Alex nodded, offering his silent approval.

There was no activity outside, at least none that we could detect. My guess was that the blaring security siren had scared the living bejeezus out of whoever it was, but I wasn't ready to test my theory until either the cops or Carlos arrived.

"So what's with the panic room?" I asked.

Alex stood up from his chair and began pacing around to the extent pacing was possible in that small room. "Five, six years ago, I was in Mexico. We were in talks to buy a significant share of a bank down there—a deal that ended up falling through. Anyway, I was kidnapped, which actually isn't that rare. They were very professional about it, which was both scary and reassuring. They knew everything about me, including the car I'd be in, my hotel, everything. Someone must have tipped them off."

"Wow," I muttered.

"The harsh part was that they not only threatened to kill *me* if they didn't get the ransom, they threatened to get my wife, too. So the bank paid them off, and now we have insurance for that kind of thing. Anyway, when that ordeal was over, my wife hired the most expensive contractor in the county to install this room. I guess it's finally paying off."

"We'll see," I said. "Pretty impressive, though," I mused.

"What, the room?" he asked.

"No. I mean to be *kidnapped*. That's big stuff. I don't think most people are worthy of being kidnapped."

He smiled at my lame attempt to lighten the mood.

The knock at the door surprised us. "Police!" a voice yelled, though the sound was muffled. "All clear!"

We looked at each other, both thinking the same thing. It had only been about three minutes since we'd called 9-1-1. Could the cops really have arrived that quickly?

"What's your name, officer?" Alex asked, raising his voice enough to pierce the five-inch door.

There was a pause, ever so slight. "Jackson," the voice said firmly as though trying to convince itself that it was true.

I was shaking my head at Alex. It didn't add up. I went back to the phone and called 9-1-1 again. The dispatcher was very confused about why I wanted to know the names of the officers being sent to the scene. After she finally understood what I wanted, I gave her the number printed on the phone and told her to call back when she found out.

In the meantime, Alex had asked the voice what his badge number was. He had rattled off five numbers, and I cursed myself that I didn't know how many numbers the LVPD used.

It was Alex's turn to shake his head. "My problem is that it's just one guy," he said. "If he was actually a cop, there'd be more than one of them."

"All clear," the voice repeated. "You can come out now."

I had a momentary flash of inspiration. "We can't!" I yelled.

Alex looked at me funny, but I held up a finger to silence him.

"Why not?"

"We've lost the code," I explained.

I explained to Alex that I didn't want the guy to think we were too suspicious or else he might get away. "The longer he lingers out there, the greater chance the cops can get him."

"Or your bouncer friend," Alex added, nodding along.

The voice had gone silent, apparently pondering the unexpected news about the missing code. It didn't make a lot of sense that there'd be a code to get *out* of a panic room, but I was betting that he'd never had any experience with one. And he had to be nervous, which meant he probably wasn't thinking straight.

"Can you look it up?" he finally asked.

I looked at Alex, who shrugged at me. Apparently, this was my show now. "That's what I'm doing now," I yelled.

"Maybe that will buy us another minute or two," I said to Alex, using a whisper that was unnecessary.

"I like your idea, though," Alex said softly. "Keeping him outside the panic room is smart. Otherwise, he gets away and tries this again sometime."

"Thanks," I said. "That's the idea, anyway. If I'm him, though, I'm going to get real squeamish pretty soon. He should suspect something is up, that we're not buying his story about being a cop."

The phone inside rang. Alex and I looked at each other.

I answered, and the dispatcher on the other end told us two squad cars were sent to the house containing officers named Krawcheck, Sloane, Manterelli, and Rodriguez. I thanked her and relayed the information that someone posing as an Officer Jackson was lingering outside the panic room.

"How far away was your friend?" Alex asked.

"Not that far," I answered. "And Carlos drives fast."

The voice from outside piped up again. "The grounds are secure," it said. "We found evidence of an intruder, who is being taken into custody. We need your help in identifying her," he explained.

"He's upping the ante," I said. "But he doesn't know we know the names of the real officers."

Alex nodded. "Information asymmetry," he said, smiling, and then he began pacing again. He was scratching his chin plaintively, probably wondering what the hell he had gotten himself into. It wasn't hard to imagine his thought process. *I go out with a stripper* one time, *and I wind up in a panic room with two squad cars on the way.*

Just then, we heard a thud and something that sounded like a scuffle. It was impossible to make anything out given the thickness of the door, but my mind's eye pictured Carlos sneaking up on the guy and putting him into a chokehold, his massive biceps pressing against the guy's face. But then a shot rang out and then another. And then there was silence.

Alex and I looked at each other, our faces mirroring looks of concern.

"What the hell are we supposed to do now?" I asked.

"We're the only ones with a safe room," he said. "I think we stay here until we have more information."

"But…" I trailed off, my mind drifting to Carlos. The silence was oppressive, gnawing away at me. "If Carlos had shot the guy, he'd let us know. But instead, there's nothing."

Alex nodded hesitantly. I could sense in him a reluctance to stick his neck out for a stranger. Our only trump card was the panic room, and if we opened the door, we'd have nothing. It was a very sensible approach.

"What was that sound?" I yelled through the door.

There was no answer.

# CHAPTER TWENTY-THREE

---

"Are you still out there?" I yelled again. "Officer Jackson?" It seemed silly to continue the ruse, but I did it anyway.

Again, there was no response.

"Do you think he's trying to bait us out there?" Alex asked. "Playing on our curiosity?"

I shrugged, annoyed by the fact that neither of us had any idea what had taken place directly outside the room only a few feet away from us. *If I ever built a panic room*, I thought, *I'd put a camera outside*.

I stood up and started pacing, and that's when the faintest sound of sirens made their muffled way into the room.

"You hear that?" Alex asked.

I nodded solemnly. "We should have our answer in a minute or two. We told them where the room is, although they might want to check the rest of the property first."

He shot me a questioning look.

"I mean, they have to make sure the entire property is secure," I said. "As long as we're safe inside here, they'll come here last."

He nodded distractedly. The two of us sat down on the floor, silently counting the seconds. If Alex was anything like me, his mind was playing out a million scenarios, most of which were not very pleasant. I couldn't help picturing Carlos lying in a pool of his own blood right outside our door, getting killed simply because I'd asked him to come help me. I had never felt guilty about playing upon his emotions, and particularly his lust, but now things were different.

I tried to shake myself out of it, tried to convince myself that there were dozens of scenarios that didn't involve Carlos getting himself shot. I knew that I had a bad habit of jumping to the worst-case scenario, so I tried to laugh it off. Deep breaths. Breathe in, hold, exhale. It wasn't working.

The seconds turned into minutes. The sirens were still audible. But were they closer or still off in the distance? It was impossible to tell.

And then the phone rang again.

"Hello?" I answered, gingerly.

It was the dispatcher. She said the police had cleared the scene and that it was safe to come out. I placed the phone back on the receiver and turned around to face Alex.

"Let's go," I said. "That was the all clear."

Just as Alex put his hand on the door, a voice rang out from the other side. "You can come out now," it said. It was authoritative in a way that the other voice hadn't been. Alex nodded at me, and he turned the handle.

A whoosh of air broke the seal as he pushed through the door. Following him out, my eyes darted everywhere, scanning the ground for signs of Carlos. The room was empty.

I exhaled, a sense of relief rushing through me.

"He's not here," I whispered.

Alex shrugged it off, unaware of the mental anguish I'd been going through for the last five minutes.

Officer Sloane, a wiry thirtysomething with gray flecks in his bristly short hair, cleared his throat. "We're sweeping the outside now, trying to see if there are any others. We've got one suspect now, though, and he's out of it. Medical situation."

I perked up. "Where is he?"

Sloane raised an eyebrow. "Ma'am, it's best if we all stay down here right now."

"Is he a Latino man, pretty muscular?" I asked.

He cocked his head to the side. "Yes, actually. Why do you—"

I brushed past Officer Sloane and rushed out of the room. A female officer was kneeling next to a body, a muscular, dark-skinned body.

"He's not the guy!" I screamed. "He came here to help us," I said, my voice trailing off. I knelt down to check on Carlos. He was breathing, but it was labored and scratchy. I couldn't help noticing the blood on the carpet underneath him.

Officer Sloane and Alex joined us, their faces a mixture of concern and annoyance.

I shot a look at the female officer who returned it with a stern, cautionary gaze. It wasn't improving my mood.

"Where was he shot?" I asked.

"Looks like somewhere near the lung," she said. "Paramedics are on the way."

"Can you tell them to step on it?" I asked.

"They always step on it," she said, trying to sound reassuring.

"But they think this is the bad guy. If you tell them he's a good guy..." I trailed off again, knowing I sounded desperate.

Alex leaned over and placed a gentle hand on my shoulder. "We'll find whoever did this," he said, his voice flinty.

Just then Carlos let out a low moan. His head turned slightly, and he opened one eye. I took it as a good sign. He seemed dazed, which was understandable, and then his one eye seemed to focus in on me. To reassure him, I tried to look like I wasn't totally freaked out, but I was never much of an actress.

"He got away," Carlos wheezed. And then his eyes shut again, a deep breath escaping his lips.

My eyes got big, and I tugged at Officer Krawcheck's sleeve. She flashed me a thin smile.

"He's just resting," she said halfheartedly. "He's still got a pulse."

I stood up, and Alex came over to put his arms around me. It was the most physical contact we'd ever had, and I couldn't help feeling bad for him that it was coming under these circumstances.

Officers Sloane and Krawcheck huddled together, with Sloane occasionally checking his radio. After about ten minutes of wondering where the ambulance was, we finally heard loud steps shuffling down the stairs. Two stocky men of almost identical build carried a stretcher and some other equipment into the room. They took a quick peek at Carlos, who was still breathing softly, and then began their solemn business.

"He tried to help us," I said, my voice cracking.

The one closer to me just nodded somberly. Wearing rubber gloves, they carefully slid the stretcher under the side of his body, being careful not to jar him too much. One of them began probing Carlos' back, presumably for an exit wound, but came up empty. When they got him onto the stretcher, they carefully lifted him up using their legs to lift and moved him out of the room. I didn't want to watch, but I was transfixed.

In the ambulance, they stuck him with a needle and started an IV. They had been completely silent the whole time, which didn't give me any confidence.

"How's he doing?" I asked.

The two looked at each other, deciding which one would speak.

"It depends where the bullet is," he said. "The surgeon will have to make the final call."

"What do you mean, the '*final call*'?" I asked, growing even more concerned.

"The bullet went in near his heart, and it's still in there," he explained. "Sometimes, it's just too close to do anything about. Removing it would sever all kinds of arteries, and somebody could never recover from that. But I'm not a surgeon or anything. I've just seen my share of gunshot wounds."

I nodded, knowing they had more important things to do than chat about surgery with a half-dressed stripper. They strapped Carlos down and then started closing the doors. I snuck one last look inside. Carlos looked pale.

The ambulance pulled away. As it turned onto the street, the lights came on. I noticed a few neighbors outside, bundled up against the crisp desert night, seeing what all the hubbub was about. It wasn't every day that two squad cars and an ambulance pulled into a neighborhood like this.

Officer Sloane had been waiting behind us, giving us a little space. He cleared his throat, and we turned around to face him.

"So if your friend wasn't the guy, obviously we've got a problem," he said matter-of-factly.

Alex nodded. "You think we should get back inside."

"I do," Sloane said. "It would be crazy for anyone to do anything to you with four of us out here, but why take the chance?" He motioned with his arm to usher us back inside. In the distance, I heard the siren of Carlos' ambulance fire up as it hit the main street.

Almost out of habit, we meandered back downstairs to the room next to the panic room. At first, it seemed comforting to be underground, but then I remembered we were in the place that Carlos had been shot. It wasn't very safe for *him*.

Sloane and Krawcheck had accompanied us downstairs, and I gathered that the other two officers were conducting some sort of search on the premises outside. Alex's lot was probably only a half acre, but someone could be hiding out in the conservancy or even in the desert that stretched up into the hills.

Sloane got a beep on his radio and listened.

"They've called in the chopper," he said.

"Do they have infrared on there?" Alex asked.

Sloane nodded. "It's perfect for something like this. Middle of the night, suspect on the loose trying to hide. They'll see his heat no matter where he is. Especially since it's only about forty degrees outside right now."

We made small talk with Sloane for a few minutes. Officer Krawcheck wasn't much of a talker, it seemed. She was about my age and had a sweet face, but she kept to herself and stood stiff, taking her role as our protector more seriously than Sloane did.

Sloane received another message on his radio. As he held it up to his ear, I studied his expression. It didn't change. Keeping his stony demeanor, he said, "We got him."

Alex and I looked at each other and smiled. "That's a relief," I said, stating the obvious.

"Did they say who it was?" Alex asked.

Sloane nodded. "Only said it was a man, white guy in his forties. We'll see soon enough, I guess."

Sloane and Krawcheck led us back upstairs where we waited outside on Alex's front porch. Within a minute, the other squad pulled up. Two officers got out, leaving the suspect in the back. I couldn't see much from where I was standing, so I moved closer.

"Recognize that guy?" Sloane asked.

I looked at Alex. "Not really." The guy in the back of the car had a sour expression on his face, which was understandable. He looked mildly creepy, with a sallow face, puffy cheeks, and thinning black hair.

The officers chatted for a moment. "Call off the chopper," Krawcheck said. "No need to wake up any more people than we already have."

Alex and I thanked the other two officers, and then they drove away to book the guy.

Sloane and Krawcheck were getting ready to leave. "He's denying it, of course," Sloane said, off-handedly. "They always do."

"Denying what?" I asked.

"Shooting anyone. But we'll run the tests. The gunshot residue test doesn't lie," he said confidently.

Alex thanked them again, and they turned and headed to their squad car, which was parked out on the street. I knew they'd spend the rest of their shift filling out paperwork.

"Well," I said, "I've got to get to the hospital. I'll call you tomorrow."

Alex shook his head. "I'll come too," he said. "Remember, you don't have a car."

"Oh, yeah," I said, feeling more than a little stupid.

We got in Alex's car, and he sped off to the closest hospital, which was called Wheaton Memorial. It wasn't a megahospital with a huge trauma center, but it seemed big enough that they would know what they were doing in the emergency room. I was happy to let Alex take charge. He grilled the intake nurse about Carlos, and she finally relented and went personally to find out how he was doing. When she returned, she said he was in surgery. There was nothing that could be done for now, so we should go home and come back the next day. The surgery could take another four to six hours, she said.

We pondered what to do. Alex politely offered to stay with me, if that's what I wanted. I was divided. My heart said stay, but the rest of me was opposed. We had been up half the night, and Alex had to work the next morning, of course. And since I didn't have my car, he was stuck with me. I didn't feel like dragging him into this any more than I already had done, and there didn't seem to be much point in staying. I would return the next morning, refreshed by a little sleep. Hopefully.

Alex and I got back in his car, and he started driving in the direction of his house. My apartment on the Strip was a good twenty minutes away, and his place was only five minutes, so it made some sense. Still, I found it interesting that he didn't take me back to my house. I was too jacked up with emotions to say anything.

We pulled into his driveway and then found ourselves in his kitchen. It felt eerie being back there.

"How are we supposed to get back to sleep?" I asked Alex.

He shrugged. "Who says we have to?"

I could tell he didn't mean the question in a suggestive way, although that's naturally how my mind interpreted it.

"You have two sets of headphones, I assume?" I asked.

He nodded. "Of course."

"Pick an album," I said. "I'll make some coffee."

He nodded, a faint smile appearing on his face.

# CHAPTER TWENTY-FOUR

————

I'm not sure what time I had clunked out, but the sharp pain in my neck told me I had been sleeping for a while. When I came to, my head was bobbed forward, like it did when I slept on an airplane, and my arm was slung over the side of a soft recliner where I'd been listening to Mahler's Second Symphony along with Alex. An incredibly soft blanket was doing its best to keep me warm. It was a miracle there wasn't a pool of drool all over it.

I pulled the headphones off and looked around. Alex was gone. He'd probably gone off to his comfortable bed, the kind of thing an intelligent person would do. I got up and stretched and then made my way up the stairs, massaging the back of my neck with my fingers. It wasn't working.

Alex was sitting at the kitchen table with a steaming cauldron of coffee, poring over the *Wall Street Journal*. He perked up when he saw me. I couldn't help wondering if this was a flash-forward, if this was how we'd greet each other every morning. Coffee, a newspaper—a *real* newspaper—the smell of fried eggs wafting through the room, a warm smile from Alex, and me feeling like I'd been run over by a truck. It sounded about right, somehow.

"Some night," he said, folding up the newspaper for future consumption.

I nodded, stifling a yawn. I must have been ogling his giant mug of coffee because he sprung up and poured some for me into an equally grand goblet. I looked at it skeptically, not sure I was up for a thousand milligrams of caffeine.

Alex sensed my hesitation. "Drink up," he said. "Coffee's good for you."

"Is it, now?" I asked wryly.

Alex started fussing around in the kitchen as though he was about to make me breakfast.

"I'll do it," I said. "You're all dressed for work." Somehow, in spite of our crazy evening, he had managed to look like a million bucks at seven in the morning, with his tailored white shirt and gray slacks, red power tie, and tan belt.

He yielded the kitchen to me and then disappeared upstairs. I made myself some eggs and then cleaned up.

I realized he probably needed to get to the office soon, and since I didn't have a key, I should skedaddle as soon as possible so he could lock up and go. I figured an Uber car would cost me twenty-five bucks to get home.

Alex reappeared in the kitchen, now with his gray suit coat on.

"You could be a model in one of those catalogs," I said, smiling.

"Which one?" he asked. "Sears?"

I brushed him off. "No, a good one. Like Brooks Brothers or something."

He shook his head, uncomfortable with the compliment. "You can stay as long as you like. I can lock up the house with my phone," he explained, patting his side pocket. "But I've got a meeting in a half hour, so I've got to run. Oh, and here's a set of keys for the Land Rover." He pointed to a key fob on the countertop.

"Oh," I said. "I can just get a car. But thanks!"

He looked confused. "What do you mean, just 'get a car'?"

Sometimes I forgot that Alex was a touch older than I was. "I have an app on my phone. I press about two buttons, and a car shows up and takes me wherever I want."

He nodded skeptically. "I think I've heard my secretary talk about that. Anyway, the Land Rover's yours for the day if you want it."

This is when it got awkward. The scene was so domestic that I felt like I was supposed to kiss him good-bye. I was sitting there, half dressed, while he was the corporate warrior going off to do battle. I stood up to face him, and he leaned in to plant a delicate little kiss on my cheek. It was very sweet, the perfect thing to do under the circumstances.

"I'll call you later," he said and headed out into the garage.

I let out a big sigh and checked the clock. It was almost eight, which meant Carlos might be out of surgery soon. It was tempting to lounge around Alex's mansion all morning, trying out the different hot tubs, but I knew I wouldn't be able to relax. I needed to check on Carlos.

The Uber driver picked me up twenty minutes later. I was relieved to find the driver to be a model of discretion. I was quite a sight, I knew, a disheveled stripper needing a morning pickup from a house I obviously didn't live in. The whole thing screamed one-night stand or, in Vegas, call girl. But the driver drove away as if I was the most boring fare he'd had in weeks.

"How'd you get past the security gates?" I asked.

"You just flash your Uber tag and they let you through. We come into these places *all* the time now." His tone of voice was only mildly suggestive, which I interpreted as a hint that rich guys commonly used Uber to drive their dates home.

At home, I showered and changed into a comfortable outfit suitable for spending the day at a hospital. Yoga pants, athletic top, and a giant thermos of coffee, which was so crucial that it might as well have been part of my outfit.

The waiting room was an interesting place. There were people there who just looked flat-out bored intermixed with a few folks who looked like they were dying of anxiety, as though another minute of waiting would put them over the edge into a full-blown panic attack. I waited in line for a minute and then spoke with the intake receptionist. She was unusually friendly, an island of warmth in an otherwise bleak environment, and promised to check on Carlos for me. I found a seat and began scanning the room, trying to make it seem like I *wasn't* scanning the room.

She saw me right away and made a little sour face. It was Carlos' on-again-off-again girlfriend. They had lived together even when no longer dating—according to *him*, anyway—as a matter of convenience and economics. She had never liked me, even though I was paying Carlos good money to help me with my work. Rightly or wrongly, she saw me as a threat, and now here I was at the hospital. And on top of all that, now I was responsible for Carlos getting shot.

I pretended not to recognize her and busied myself with my phone for a few minutes. When the woman from the front desk came, I stood up.

"Everything went well," she said. "The bullet punctured his lung and caused a lot of bleeding, but they were able to repair most of it."

I smiled, fighting back the tears that began running down my cheeks. "So he's going to be okay?"

"The doctors are cautiously optimistic," she said, patting me on the shoulder. "But you won't be able to see him for a while, unfortunately. Family only." My pale skin and lack of a wedding ring made it obvious that I wasn't family, I supposed. "But he won't be saying much for a few days, anyway."

"All right," I said. "Thank you very much."

I watched the nurse walk over to Carlos' sometime girlfriend, who stood up and accompanied the nurse back into the hospital. Before the doors closed behind her, she shot me a look. *I win,* she was saying.

*Bitch,* I thought. She wasn't family either, I knew, but she must have talked her way in. *Big deal*, I thought. When he was back on his feet, Carlos would still prefer me.

I tried to shake out of it on my drive home. I had just received great news about Carlos, but instead of appreciating that news, I was caught up in a morass of jealousy about the fact that his girlfriend—if that's what she was, this week—got to visit him but I didn't. It wasn't fair. The rational part of my brain knew that my inability to visit him was just a tiny blip on the radar screen of life, but it was still bugging me to no end.

And then I laughed at my childishness. As a kid, I could ignore one of my dolls for weeks at a stretch, but as soon as my sister picked it up, it became my new obsession. I *had* to have it. The same, apparently, was true with men. Carlos had practically been throwing himself at me for years, and with one exception, I'd never reciprocated. But now that someone else was getting to visit him, I wanted to see him more than ever.

Back in my apartment, I caught up on some sleep and tried to distract myself from thoughts of Carlos. Why did things have to be so complicated? I had just gotten closer to Alex who was suddenly an available and eligible man, and now I found myself pining for Carlos who had been there all along. I wondered if men suffered through such dilemmas or if everything just came easily to them. I suppose it must be easy when all you cared about was one thing.

Thinking of Alex, I began wondering what the police had done with the guy they'd arrested at Alex's house. Had Owen really sent him there to kill me or just to threaten me, or did he have some other nefarious purpose?

I was getting antsy. Even if the police had taken care of that threat, I still had the problem of Dan's wife, Laura. The last I'd heard, she was still missing. I called Dan to check in, and he confirmed the news.

"The police have started a file on her, whatever that means," he said.

"It means about what you expect," I said. He was smart, and I didn't need to sugarcoat it for him. "Basically, in domestic cases like this, they give people a wide berth. If a twelve-year-old goes missing, they run a full-court press. But when a grown woman ups and leaves, they're not going to bust their asses looking for her."

"That's about what I figured," he said. "Frankly, it's kind of embarrassing. She left me, and that's all there is to it."

"She left the kids, too," I added. "There must have been something going on. I'll keep working on it, if that's what you want."

"Thanks, Raven. I'd really like to find her. Even if it's just to know where she is and why she left."

When I hung up, it struck me how far afield Dan's case had gone. It had started with trying to find out who was stealing money from their blackjack group, but then I had gotten myself drugged by a sleazy minister, and the client's wife had disappeared. All in all, I was a human wrecking ball, bringing destruction and chaos wherever I ended up.

As I was making lunch, the valet called up to tell me my car had been delivered. *Alex was* good, I thought. A guy who could make things happen. After lunch, I forced myself to tackle the problem of finding Dan's wife. I had never worked on a missing-persons case before, and I sympathized with the cops' laid-back attitude in circumstances like this. If his wife wanted to split, which is apparently the case, there wasn't any crime to investigate. I was tempted to call up an acquaintance who happened to run the largest private investigation firm in town. I had worked with Philippe Lagarde on a case a couple of months earlier, and the resources his company had were incredible. He could probably track Laura down in a matter of hours, or days. But Dan had hired *me* to do it, and I could use the experience, especially since Las Vegas was one of the missing-persons capitals of the world. People come here, get entranced by all the flashing lights and slot machines, and then disappear after they lose all their money.

My first stop would be Dan's neighbors. They might have seen something around the time she left, and they might even have spoken with Laura on her way out. From my experience, just showing up at someone's house at three in the afternoon wasn't usually very productive. People were in school or had jobs. So I spent the rest of the day making a double batch of chili—enough food for a family of eight—and then headed over to Dan's neighborhood around five.

Las Vegas traffic is bad at almost every hour, but five o'clock was noticeably worse. I finally arrived at Dan's street, where I did a slow drive-by and then parked at the end of the block. The early evening sun was halfway through its descent, the air still dry and hot but not hot enough to keep a young mom and her son from frolicking around with a soccer ball.

I approached the woman and held out a business card. She was wary, like most people, that I wanted to sell her something she didn't need. I explained the situation, asking if she'd seen or heard anything, but she was blank.

"You might try two doors down," she said, pointing at a larger pink stucco ranch. "They're pretty close, I think. We just moved in last year, so we don't know everyone," she explained.

I thanked her and moved along to the next house, which was three down from Dan's. It looked pretty dead, but I rang the bell anyway. It came up a blank. The mom next door was watching me closely but trying to make it look like she wasn't. I supposed it wasn't every day that a private investigator showed up in a nice little suburb like this.

The pink stucco ranch had matching pink rocks in the front yard and a bluestone walkway leading up to the front door. The shades were all drawn, so I couldn't see anything inside. I rang the bell and waited. Once more. Just as I was turning on my heel to leave, the door opened a crack. It was a small girl of about seven. She didn't say anything but just stood there staring at me.

I began to ask if her mom or dad were around when a tall, thin woman in her thirties appeared behind the girl and fixed me with a stare that could not be described as friendly and welcoming. She wore a tight ponytail and looked like she was about to go jogging. I appreciated that people didn't like being disturbed by strangers at the door, but most of them hid their displeasure behind a smiling mask. She didn't feel the need to bother, apparently.

The woman shooed the girl away and stared at my business card. When I explained my very modest mission, she seemed to soften a hair.

"She's missing?" she asked, sounding genuinely concerned. "I swear, I thought I just saw her a couple of days ago. Or maybe it was three," she mused.

I nodded. "She's only been gone a few days, so that would make sense. What we're trying to get a handle on is whether she left voluntarily, or whether…" I trailed off, not wanting to give voice to the unlikely but unpleasant alternative.

"They weren't happy, if that's what you're asking," the woman said after a brief moment of contemplation. I sensed she had decided to cut to the chase as the most effective means of getting rid of me quickly.

"Right," I said. "I'm wondering if you saw anything, though. Or if she said anything specific about leaving. People leave all the time, especially in Vegas. But when there are kids involved, it's much rarer."

She nodded thoughtfully. "Especially for the woman. There are days when I *want* to leave, but there's just no way." She had been staring past me into the street, but then our eyes met, and I sensed she felt she had revealed too much about her own life.

"That's why Dan's concerned," I said. "It would be completely out of character."

"Well, like I said, I thought I saw her just the other day. And she hasn't said anything to me, so I don't think I can be very helpful. I could reach out to her, I suppose. Send her a text or something. Would that help?"

I nodded, wondering why I hadn't thought of it. "I was just about to suggest that," I lied. "You've got my business card, so please let me know if you hear anything from her." I offered my hand, and the woman shook it. As I left, it occurred to me then that I hadn't even asked her name or gotten her cell number. It was a failing I filed away among the countless others with the hope that in time I'd learn.

There was no activity at Dan's house. Only one of the other neighbors was home, and he hadn't seen or heard anything, either about Laura in particular or about the couple's relationship in general. I offered him my business card, which he brushed off but then, upon reconsideration, decided to take. From the creepy vibe he was giving off, I assumed he was going to go Google my name and do a little cyber stalking. As I drove back home, the lingering doubt began creeping back into my thoughts. I was leaving a lucrative job as a stripper mainly because I hated dealing with creeps, but I was replacing that job with a less lucrative one that also required dealing with creeps. I shook my head at myself and looked in the rearview mirror.

"Only you," I said to my reflection. "Only *you* would do something like this."

# CHAPTER TWENTY-FIVE

———

I had resolved to wake up before noon, but I didn't recover as quickly as I used to from a night of dancing until three. Noon came and went unnoticed. By one o'clock, I was rolling around under the sheets, fighting the reality of another day at the office. I had to find Dan's wife, and then I had to go back to Cougar's to cash in on the Friday night crowd. A little voice inside me told me I wouldn't have to do any of that if I married Alex. I could sleep in as long as I wanted, roll out of bed whenever I wanted, and have a cook fix me eggs, sausage, and bacon, extra crispy. Well, the cook part was a stretch. Alex was too down-to-earth to hire servants. But still. If *I* was the lady of the house…

I shook myself out of it and made a pot of coffee, the effects of which I didn't sufficiently feel until the third cup. I didn't even kid myself that I'd go to the gym. Hemming and hawing about whether or not to go would have wasted precious time, especially since the answer would always end up a resounding *no*. By two o'clock, I got my car at the valet and headed across town to the place where Laura worked. I figured she would have friends there, someone she could have confided in before she left.

Laura's employer was a technology company housed in the top two floors of a tan four-story office building. The building was part of an office park that encircled an oval green space with a small park and palm trees galore. There was a receptionist's desk at the entry, but it was occupied only by a pair of ferns and a sign directing visitors to the building directory on the wall.

I took the stairs up, peering into the large windows at all of the worker bees going about their daily business. By the third floor, I had convinced myself that my jobs weren't so bad after all. I couldn't imagine myself dressing in business casual every day and filling out reports or giving sales presentations as if any of that stuff mattered. I wanted to be on my feet, moving around and seeing the world, not cooped up in some cubicle taking orders from a guy with a night-school MBA. But then again, I had a way to rationalize just about anything.

The Tech-Chron Corporation made software for the gambling industry, but apart from that I knew nothing about it. They didn't exactly have a receptionist at the entryway, but a plump woman with pink cheeks said hello to me, so I pounced.

She examined my business card and then gave me the once-over.

"Are you the famous one?" she asked, left eyebrow raised.

I smiled and tried to brush it off. "Not exactly. I was in the news a few months ago, but that's it."

The woman gushed with delight. In the old days, I had often been recognized as the girl from the giant billboards plastered around town. I supposed being recognized as a detective was a mild upgrade.

"My name's Gloria," she said. "Can I keep this?" She asked, fingering my business card. There was a twinkle in her eye.

"Uh, sure. Anyway, I'm here about Laura Hartmann. Her husband is concerned about her and has hired me to investigate."

She nodded solemnly. Her desire to cooperate was palpable. "What can I tell you?" She asked. Then she looked back and forth to see if anyone was within earshot. Before I could answer, she began whispering in a conspiratorial voice. "Nobody really likes her, if you want to know the truth," she said.

I nodded, stone-faced, trying not to laugh. "And why is that?" I asked, pretending to be very concerned.

The woman looked around again to make sure she wasn't being overheard. "Because she sneaks other people's treats. One time, I brought in a whole plate of pumpkin spice muffins, and before ten, the plate was half empty! And there were *crumbs* on her desk! I saw them myself."

I had to stifle a laugh at the image of the rotund and rosy-faced Gloria sleuthing around the office with a giant magnifying glass, hunting for incriminating crumbs.

"And treats are serious business, right?" I asked.

"Oh yes," she said solemnly. "That's not why you're here, though, is it?"

Um, no, I thought. I'm not here about muffins, scones, donuts, or any kind of pastry whatsoever. "I'm here because she's gone missing."

"Oh, right," she said, looking a bit foolish. "That was a little scary, wasn't it?"

"*Was*?" I asked.

She nodded. "I mean, we were very glad to see her back at work the next day. Even though we didn't like her very much." She said this last part in her trademark whisper.

I was confused. "Wait. You're saying she's *back* at work?"

"Oh yes," she said. "She was out on Tuesday, but she's been back ever since."

"And is she here now?" I asked.

"Let me check. Here, come with me." She led me through a maze of gray cubicles, many of which were covered with a spaghetti of bright-colored wires and power cords. Most of the employees seemed to be men in their twenties and thirties, more than a few of whom seemed to be trying to check me out without wanting to be obvious about it. But they were. I winked at one guy, a chubby balding man of about thirty-five, and I blew a kiss to a younger Indian guy. Both of them immediately stared down at the floor. I swear, even the Indian guy's dark-skinned face had developed a reddish hue. Ah, nerds.

Apparently, Laura was hot stuff because she had an office with a view rather than a cubicle in nerdville. The office was empty.

Gloria shot a questioning look at an older woman in the office next door.

"She's out at a client call this afternoon. Probably not coming back today," the woman said.

I thanked Gloria for her help and, on a whim, decided to give her a few extra business cards. "Tell your friends," I said. She was delighted.

I got back in my car, turned on the air conditioning, and just sat there. So, Laura was back, as though nothing had happened. And she'd *been* back, too. It wasn't a recent development, and yet Dan had just asked me to keep looking for her. That meant one of two things. Either Dan *knew* she was back and wanted me to look for her anyway, which would be strange. Or she hadn't told Dan that she was back and was staying somewhere else. At least she'd be easy to find now, I figured. I could just call Dan and tell him she was okay and was continuing to work at Tech-Chron.

But that raised another question with me. I had assumed that Laura had run off with Owen, but would she continue to stay with him now that he'd been arrested? Women were funny like that, I knew. They could stick with their man no matter what, but this was a big *what*.

And that reminded me that I hadn't heard anything about the case against Owen lately. I stopped by the grocery store on my way home and picked up some fixings to make a giant salad, which ended up being more shredded cheese than shredded lettuce. And then I called Tricia from the DA's office. It was four o'clock on a Friday, so it was a long shot.

A secretary answered and then put me right through.

"Hi Raven," Tricia said. Her voice was cheerful enough, although to my jaded ear it sounded forced.

"So what's next?" I asked.

"I was just going to call you, actually," she said. That got my hackles up. Whenever someone said "actually" to me, I assumed the person was lying. "There's been a development."

*Here we go,* I thought. "Did he accept a plea?"

"It's in the works. Should be signed on Monday," she said vaguely.

"How much jail time?" I asked, trying to cut to the chase.

"Four years, plus two years of supervision and mandatory sexual assault counseling. Plus a stiff fine," she added. "That's our joint recommendation, anyway. It'll be up to the judge."

I sighed. I was a big girl and didn't want to make a stink about it, so I just rolled over. "So that's it, then?"

She was silent for a moment. "It's a solid deal," she said softly. "He's a first time offender, so it's hard to get a lot of prison time unless the case is rock solid. A lot of drug dealers get less than four years." For some reason, I felt bad for Tricia. She knew it was a crappy deal and that she'd let me down and that in four years, Owen would be free to do the same thing to another woman.

"I think I understand," I said, resigned. "Let me know if there's anything more you need from me."

I was staring out my window, doing nothing, and I'm not sure if I stood there for ten minutes or a half hour. I didn't know what I was really expecting. The death penalty? Twenty years? Four years wasn't enough, though. Intellectually, I knew he'd hired a top lawyer, and I also knew that I wasn't exactly the most compelling victim. Detective Goss had hinted at the possibility, and now it was clear he was right. Would a jury ever sympathize with a stripper? Would they think I led him on? Even in Vegas, strippers were sometimes second-class citizens. Especially when the accused was a popular and powerful minister.

# CHAPTER TWENTY-SIX

———

On Saturday morning, my phone roused me out of a restless sleep. It was Laura Hartmann.

"Raven, I'm in trouble," she said, her voice a little shaky.

She and I had barely spoken before, so I wondered why or how she was calling me.

"What's going on?" I asked, squinting at the clock next to my bed. It was just after eleven.

"Well, I left Dan. Actually, I was *taken* away from him. Two guys I don't know abducted me and took me to a small house where they locked me in the crawl space under the house."

"Wow," I said, not believing a word of it. "Are you still there?"

"Kind of. I broke out, and now I'm in the house. They just left. Can you help me?" Her voice had a twinge of desperation in it.

I didn't know how to answer. My mind was spinning, trying to make sense of it all. Obviously, she didn't know that I'd already visited her office, which meant I knew she hadn't been abducted by some strange men. So why was she asking for my help? I decided to stall for time.

"Where are you?" I asked.

"The address outside says 7113, but I can't tell what street I'm on."

"Are you on your own phone?" I asked.

She thought for a second. "Yes. They left it in the house after they took it from me."

"Then it should have a map on there, where you can get your location," I said, playing along.

She pretended to fiddle with her phone for a few seconds, as though pulling up the app. "Okay, here it is, Raven. It says I'm on Sagebrush Court."

I wrote down the address. "Can you get away?" I asked. I was wondering why she thought she needed my help, why she couldn't just walk away on her own.

Laura paused for a minute. She seemed to be making it up as she went along, probably on the assumption that I'd just drop everything and come to her rescue without giving it a second thought. "I'm really too scared to do anything, Raven. The second I leave, they'll probably come back and find me. And then, they'd probably start beating me again."

I rolled my eyes, but I kept playing along because I wanted to see where she was going with this. "Okay, stay put. I'll be there as soon as I can."

"Oh, thank you, Raven! Please hurry." Her voice sounded relieved.

After I hung up, I made a large pot of coffee, hoping that a few cups of java would jump-start my caffeine-deprived brain. Even though Laura was expecting me to hurry, she couldn't possibly expect me to come to her fake rescue without any coffee in my system.

After half a cup, the mental fog began to lift. What the hell was Laura up to? Why call *me*, of all people, instead of simply dialing 9-1-1? It had to be some kind of setup. I wasn't keen on visiting 7113 Sagebrush Court, but on the other hand, I sensed that this was a problem that wasn't going to go away. Right now, I had the edge because I suspected a trap, and I didn't want to give that up.

The problem, I realized, was that the guy I'd normally call for help was in the hospital recovering from a gunshot wound. And I knew Mike was out of town visiting his parents in Utah. So I was flying solo, and that meant I wouldn't be flying at all. I couldn't envision any scenario in which it made sense for me to go try to "rescue" Laura from a mysterious address. What kept nagging at me was *why*. Why did they care about me? Had Laura realized that I'd linked her to the theft of money? If so, that didn't explain Dan who had continued to ask me to find Laura even after she had resurfaced. He must be involved, too, I decided. But what was the link?

And then it dawned on me. If I was right that Laura was trying to lure me into some kind of trap, it meant there would probably be no one home at their house. If I could rummage around in there while they were waiting for me at 7113 Sagebrush Court, maybe I could find something to tie everything together—an open email, a Post-it on the fridge, or even just evidence that Laura had returned home and that Dan knew it. Just about *anything* would make things clearer than they were at that moment.

I looked up 7113 Sagebrush Court and found that it was in a residential part of town about four miles from Dan's house. It was enough of a buffer zone but not by much. I dialed up the valet and found my car waiting for me when I got downstairs.

I sped over to Dan and Laura's house, making great time, and then did my usual slow drive-by when I reached his street. The house looked dead, although I could have said the same thing for most of the other houses in the neighborhood. Despite the approaching autumn season, it was still ninety degrees in the midday sun, and people tended to batten down the hatches and live their lives almost exclusively indoors.

The fact that everyone was indoors gave me a little cover since I didn't have to worry about people being outside and seeing me. There was always the chance that a neighbor would glance out her window and spot me, though, so I was hoping to be quick.

One thing I'd learned in PI school had proven true—act like you're supposed to be there, especially if you *aren't* supposed to be there. Go skulking and sneaking around, and people can sniff that out without any trouble. They have an innate sense of when things don't look right. But if you're a woman armed with a clipboard, you look nonthreatening (as a woman) and appear like you're there on official business (the clipboard). At Mike Caffrey's recommendation, I always carried a clipboard in my car just for moments like these. It made me look like I was conducting a survey or inspecting something. It gave me a mantle of legitimacy, at the very least. If someone challenged me, I'd be screwed. But the point was to avoid the challenge in the first place. If you look like you know what you're doing, like you *belong*, most people, being lazy and averse to confrontation, will leave you alone.

All of this is to explain why at high noon on a Saturday morning, you could find me walking up my client's driveway, clipboard in hand, with a businesslike expression on my face. The first thing I noticed, apart from my rapid heart rate, was the empty carport. Good. I worked my way around to the backyard and was equally pleased to see an eight-foot cinder block wall encircling the yard. I would have privacy here.

I halfheartedly tried the back door, knowing it would be locked, which it was. There were two double-hung windows at just above eye level, but they didn't budge either. I looked around to make sure no one was watching, and then I reached in my pocket and removed my driver's license. Up on my tippy-toes, I reached up and tried to slide it between the two windows, hoping I could push the latch open. It budged a half inch but then locked up, giving me the sense that if I had a ladder and something stronger than a driver's license, it would have worked perfectly.

I tried again at the second window and found success. Like the first, it had resisted my efforts after giving way slightly, but I was able to wedge my elbow against the frame and push my driver's license through. The window stuck a little, as though it hadn't been opened in a long time, but after jiggling it back and forth, it came loose and allowed me to push it up.

That was the easy part, I soon realized. The opening was certainly big enough for me to crawl through, but the problem was that it was five feet off the ground. And, although I was flexible, I was no gymnast. The perfect thing to climb on would have been an old metal garbage can, but I hadn't seen one of those in years. I scanned the barren yard, coming up empty and cursed, not for the first time. I was not going to get inside without breaking at least one nail.

I found that I was able to get a tenuous grip with my hands on the inside of the window frame, but the trouble was finding a grip with my feet. The cream-colored bricks had little valleys where the mortar held them together, of course, but it was scarcely enough to fit the toe of my sandals in. And then I sighed again as the realization struck me. I would have to go in barefoot.

I kicked off my sandals, looking around once more to make sure that no one was watching this slow-motion circus disaster. And then I tried again, pulling myself up from inside the window frame and desperately finding a grip with my toes. I finally realized that I could use the bottoms of my bare feet and not just the toes, and once I did that, I had enough leverage to push myself up and through the window.

Waiting for me on the inside was a large steel double sink filled with the obligatory pile of unwashed dishes and saucepans. Yuck. From the smell of it, someone had boiled a diseased mule and then forgotten to clean up the leftovers. There really wasn't anywhere for me to land safely, especially since I was coming in headfirst. But I didn't have the luxury of hovering there much longer since the window frame, which is all that was holding me, was digging painfully into my midsection. So I went for it, diving down in slow motion, placing my hands on the rim of the sink to slow my descent. One knee slid through, leaving that leg dangling precariously in the air, and then I pressed that leg's bare foot against the wall as I brought the other leg through.

At that point, an acrobat would have done a backflip to get out of that mess, but my only option was to kind of collapse into the sink, one limb at a time. My left knee landed in a small pan with some kind of sticky yellow sauce in it, while the other knee found its way, naturally, to a tray of something that looked like it had once been a casserole of some kind. Was that eggplant in there?

It was disgusting, but I had found a firm enough footing to allow me to crawl out of the sink onto the countertop, from which I slid down onto the floor. I found a washcloth and washed the unidentifiable food particles from my arms and legs and then threw it back in the sink. I shuddered.

Considering that it was midday, it was surprisingly dark in the kitchen. I wasn't bold enough to turn on a light or open the shades, though, so I would have to make do. As I scanned the room, it was evident that neither Dan nor Laura were clean freaks. A disheveled pile of papers lay on the kitchen table, accompanied by a sad-looking orchid in a small pot and a few mostly empty drinking glasses. I took a quick peek at the papers, but mostly it was junk mail and car insurance renewal information, nothing I was interested in.

The kitchen opened into a medium-sized living area with dated carpeting and an old upright piano standing against the wall. Plastic covers protected the sofa and a matching recliner, as though they were being preserved just in case Queen Elizabeth showed up unannounced for tea. The living room connected with the front foyer, and then beyond that lay the private side of the house, the side with the bedrooms.

There were two proper bedrooms and an office, of sorts. After a quick once-over of the bedrooms, I headed into the office and sat down at the computer desk which had a sorry-looking laptop resting on top of a few textbooks, probably for ergonomic reasons. My vague hope was that, like most people, they would have set all their browsers to remember their passwords on various websites, which would allow me to do a little snooping without having to crack any codes, something that was well beyond my skill level.

The computer was off, which wasn't promising since it suggested it might just be sitting there gathering dust. It also meant the possibility of needing a password to get into it, but when I just hit *Enter* at the prompt, it let me right through. One hurdle down.

I fired up Internet Explorer which took me to a bizarre home page that was nothing but celebrity news and gossip. It was one flashy photo after another, each accompanied by a *National Enquirer*-style headline like, "Is Trouble on the Horizon for Brad Pitt?" or "Kardashians Reveal Truth About Booty Implants." *Really?* Here I thought I had been dealing with God-fearing Christians, but apparently, they were just as materialistic and celebrity-obsessed as any other American.

I hit the jackpot on the *Favorites Bar*, which had an icon for a Yahoo! Mail link that proved to be Laura's. My first impression was that Laura was not a sophisticated user of email since most of the stuff in her main folder was spam rather than communications from actual people. The obsessive-compulsive in me was tempted to organize her email so that it wouldn't be so cumbersome and disorganized, but obviously, I didn't want to leave fingerprints.

Scanning through the dozens of emails she received every day was taking more time than I wanted. I was hoping to find some kind of smoking gun that explained why she had essentially faked her own disappearance and then tried to lure me to some kind of ambush. Was she working with Owen? With Dan? Nothing made sense.

After about five minutes, I gave up. Snooping around someone's house gave me a creepy feeling which was compounded by the fact that I was reading her emails as well, and I wanted to move on to see if I could find anything from Dan's side. There were no other email buttons on the browser, however, and none of the other email sites like Gmail and Outlook seemed to recognize the computer. I looked around in the desk to see if there was a master password sheet or anything, but it was all but empty. It seemed like my little breaking and entering trip had been a complete waste.

But there was one more shot, I realized. I closed Internet Explorer and opened up Firefox, whose icon I recognized from my own computer. It was a whole different browser which meant a whole different set of favorites and buttons. Sure enough, the Gmail site was bookmarked, and it sent me directly to Dan's inbox, no questions asked. Unlike Laura's, his was well organized by category—personal, social, promotions, and spam. There wasn't a lot in his personal directory, which made me wonder if he was an email deleter. Most people tended to keep emails forever since they didn't take up much space and because space was essentially free. I scanned the few dozen emails in his inbox and shook my head. The most interesting thing was a message from a member of the blackjack group. He had a dental emergency and wouldn't be showing up for practice that night. That was nearly two weeks ago.

I slumped back in the chair. Part of me knew going in that it was a shot in the dark, that there wasn't much chance I'd be able to find anything explaining their odd behavior, no smoking gun email or document. Even so, it bugged me that what had begun as a simple investigation about money had pitted my client and his wife against *me* with no obvious reason.

The clock was ticking, but I decided to check Dan's favorites list. Sure enough, he had a link to Southwest Trust Bank, and just as I'd hoped, the browser had saved his log-in and password information. With a couple of clicks, I was able to pull up every bank statement for the last eighteen months.

The first thing that jumped out at me was the total: $49,283.55. Who, I wondered, had forty-nine thousand bucks in a checking account? Since a checking account was drawing interest at a rate of about one one-hundredth of a percent, keeping money in there was about the equivalent of stuffing the money under your mattress. Carlos would not have approved. And then there were the direct deposits. It looked like there were two regular entries. Laura's employer deposited a few thousand bucks every two weeks, but a second deposit of five thousand even appeared every month. The payor's name was gibberish, however. The entries only read *Direct Deposit ID cfm994802490*. I checked a few other statements, and all had the identical entry on them.

I pressed the *Print Screen* key and waited, crossing my fingers that the printer was hooked up. A few seconds later, a printer hidden underneath stacks of papers whirred to life, surprised that it was being called back into action. And then it began beeping at me, an angry whine alerting me that something was wrong and that in no event should I expect a printed page to emerge from its tray in the near future.

I got down on my hands and knees, trying not to move too many things around, and found the problem. It was out of paper. I found a sheaf of paper underneath some more insurance papers and shoved a few into the feeder. Remarkably, it began firing up, and ten seconds later, I was holding a copy of their bank statement in my hands. I folded it up and placed it in my pocket, and then I got the hell out of there.

I replaced the kitchen windows to their normal positions, locked them, and then left through the kitchen door, remembering to lock it from the inside before I left. Just before I closed the door, I paused, gripped by a sense of something wrong, something I'd forgotten. I ran through a mental checklist, and then it hit me. I'd left the bank website open in Dan's browser. He probably wouldn't notice, but it wasn't good practice to leave such obvious tracks.

I made my way back to the office and turned on the monitor. Sure enough, the website had already logged me out after three minutes of activity. "For security reasons," it explained, which drew a chuckle from me. The bank's ugly logo remained in the center of the screen. I made a mental note to talk to Alex, the CEO, about getting that changed. I closed out of the browser, turned off the monitor, and returned the chair to its original place under the desk.

And that's when I heard the sirens.

*Take a deep breath*, I told myself. There are sirens in Las Vegas at all hours of the day. But I couldn't shake a suspicion that the sirens had something to do with me. This was a residential neighborhood, several blocks from any busy streets. Somebody must have seen me crawling into the kitchen window.

I ran to the front door and peered out through its narrow window. I couldn't see anything, but the sirens were definitely getting closer. It was time to get out of there, even if it meant leaving through the front door. I had rather casually committed a felony by breaking in to Dan's house, and it didn't matter that I was a private investigator. The law made no exceptions.

I was halfway out the front door when I saw the black Lexus pull up at an alarming speed. As it approached my car, the driver slammed on the brakes and pulled over, quite deftly I thought, like a man who'd had training well beyond high school Driver Ed. He was now less than twenty-five feet behind my car, meaning that I was trapped. Had the police let the guy out already? Or had they captured the wrong guy? My head was spinning, distracting me from the more important matter of what the hell I should be doing in response.

Obviously, I couldn't go out to my car now that the Lexus had cozied up to it, so I jumped back inside the house and closed the door as quickly as I could without attracting attention. The driver had probably been too busy parking his car to notice me stepping out of the door which was partially shielded by a porch. I watched through the door's narrow window.

The driver sat in his car for a few seconds, the darkened windows showing only a dim profile. All I could tell was that the driver was a large person, probably a man, who seemed to be talking on a cell phone. When the figure's hand lowered from his face, he opened his door and stepped out of the car, scanning the street and Dan's front yard before walking up to my car. He was about fifty with a gray buzz cut and aviator sunglasses, olive skin, a ramrod-straight back, and a John Wayne swagger. Ex-military, I figured.

The sirens were getting louder, but they didn't seem to bother him as he inspected my car. He was bending over now, peering through the front window, and then he leaned against it and whipped out his phone again to make a call. Why was he so interested in my car?

I tried to make sense of it. Clearly, it was not the same man the police had arrested at Alex's house, the same man who I had assumed to have shot Carlos. The guy they had arrested seemed more of a turd, and he'd denied shooting anyone despite the fact that he'd been caught trespassing on Alex's property. By contrast, the guy leaning on my car was a serious man, a guy I could easily imagine committing acts of violence. And enjoying it.

The sirens got distinctly louder, their blare no longer a vague whine but a brisk, sharp affront to the ears. And then I heard the distinct rumble of a large diesel engine as it shifted gears and gained speed. It was a fire truck, followed closely by an ambulance. They headed straight past the house, and then the truck driver stomped loudly on the brakes in front of a pink-hued stucco ranch three doors down the street.

I cringed. By now I had been hoping the police would arrive, and maybe I could concoct some story to get myself out of it. Anything was better than facing the guy outside. And why was he leaning on my car? It was almost as if he wanted me to see him. He knew I would be inside, and the blaring sirens would have lured anyone to the front windows to see what was going on. And that's when I got a deep, sinking feeling, a split-second realization that I had been duped.

It happened faster than I expected, every last gasp of air leaving my body at once, as though I had been squeezed from behind by an angry bear. I almost blacked out, but I was conscious enough to feel a couple of ribs being broken and then falling, almost lifeless, to the floor. My eyes were shut, and I was losing consciousness fast, and the last thing I heard was the unmistakable sound of duct tape being pulled and ripped off a roll.

# CHAPTER TWENTY-SEVEN

———

I don't know if it was two minutes or twelve, but it wasn't long before I came to. My brain was in a fog, and as I regained consciousness, I realized I was in a small, dark room— maybe a closet—and the weirdest thing I noticed was that I was forced to breathe through my nose. And then I felt the duct tape on my wrists, pinned uncomfortably behind my back, and I soon realized it was taped across my mouth, too. In fact, it seemed to be strapped all the way around my head, which was pressed awkwardly into a pile of laundry or towels. A fiery spot on the back of my head throbbed painfully. Instinctively, I reached up to touch it, forgetting that my hands were bound behind me.

I heard muffled voices outside, two men, which meant there were *at least* two men out there. What did they want with me? My brain was in a haze, distracted by pain and panic, but I knew it had to be Owen's doing. We'd assumed that the guy the police found on Alex's lawn was the same guy who'd been following us in the black Lexus, but obviously that had been wishful thinking. *I should have taken the reverend's money*, I thought ruefully. Why did I have to follow through with it? I didn't even like being called a "victim." I just wanted to get the guy off the street for a while so he couldn't keep doing what he was doing. Being bound and gagged, and probably killed, would be my reward.

Ten minutes went by, or was it twenty? There was an occasional gurgle of human speech outside the door, but I couldn't make anything out. It seemed like they were waiting for something. True to form, my mind was treating me to a slideshow of gruesome death images. Hanging, drugging, bludgeoning, getting shot at close range by a fifty-caliber assault rifle, getting thrown into a pool of hungry sharks, you name it. The images kept flashing through my mind. It got so bad that I began wishing for a mafia-style plug behind the ear. That would be quick and simple.

Eventually, I heard what sounded like a mini commotion outside the door. I couldn't see a thing, but I assumed I was in one of the bedroom closets because I was surrounded by clothes and soft linens. I sensed there were now a couple of extra people in the room outside the closet door, and I strained to listen.

That's when the door opened, the light from the room hurting my eyes. I squinted up to see the profile of the guy from the Lexus. He reached down and grabbed me under my arm, heaving me up with incredible strength. Pressed against him for a moment, I felt the unmistakable bulge of hard metal under his shirt. When my eyes finally adjusted to the light, I caught a glimpse of his face. He wasn't wearing a hateful, murderous expression, but one more suggestive of businesslike resignation, as though he wanted to get this over with and get paid. Maybe I was reading too much into it, but it was almost scarier that way.

Squinting into the brightness, I looked around and saw a complete stranger, a wiry but athletic man of about thirty-five who was fixing me with a pitiful stare. Bald and with olive skin and dark eyes, he looked like an Israeli commando. He must have been the one who coldcocked me from behind. I nodded at him, sarcastically, as though we were old friends getting reacquainted.

And then I noticed *them* standing in the hallway, Dan and Laura. So, they were in on this too. Both were standing awkwardly next to the door, shifting their weight around. Neither of them would make eye contact with me. Dan had originally hired me to trace where some money had gone, and now he'd turned on me. He must *really* have treasured his pastor if he was going to protect him like this. It was something I couldn't relate to. If my priest had drugged a woman and tried to assault her, I would find a new church, and I definitely wouldn't try to silence the woman who made the allegations. It was crazy.

But here we were. No one said anything, which naturally, I took as a bad sign. Executioners don't engage in a lot of chitchat before they slip the noose on, I figured. Finally, it got awkward, and the man from the Lexus loosened his grip on my arm and turned to face me.

"You've caused a lot of trouble," he said matter-of-factly. And then he carefully removed the tape from across my mouth. It hurt less than I'd expected.

"*I* didn't cause any trouble," I said, unable to stifle the protest.

The man just shook his head.

It was at that moment when I realized there was something *off* about the whole thing, something above and beyond the fact that I was standing in a stranger's house with duct tape holding my arms behind me. It was the gun. The wiry guy across the room had a gun, but it wasn't pointed at me. He was aiming at Dan and Laura. That's why they weren't looking up, I realized. It had nothing to do with the fact that they'd betrayed me. They were about to be killed themselves.

"Can somebody explain what's going on?" I asked, exasperated. If I was going to get killed, I didn't want to stand around awkwardly staring at a bunch of strangers first.

The two guys with guns looked at each other.

"There's been a change of plans," the guy next to me said vaguely. "It will be more complicated, but the result will be the same."

The *result*, I mused. *You mean my blood-spattered corpse?* I wanted to kick him in the groin, but he had just cocked his gun menacingly, so I thought better of it.

The wiry guy was inspecting the room, keeping one eye on Dan and Laura. "It would be better in the kitchen," he said to his associate, who nodded and grunted.

"Let's go," he said, giving me a gentle shove.

Both of them followed behind the three of us. I felt no love for Dan and Laura, of course, but apparently we were in the same boat. I wondered what they had done to wind up at the wrong end of a nine millimeter.

"Turn left, into the kitchen," one of them grunted behind us.

Oddly, I was calmer at that grim moment than I typically was while flying in an airplane or visiting the dentist. Dan and Laura were both ashen faced, their postures slumped in resignation. They'd been defeated, but I still wondered why, and how.

"You, there," the Lexus guy said, pointing with his gun. He was directing me towards the kitchen table.

"You two, stand closer, over there," he said, speaking to Dan and Laura. His voice retained its businesslike tone, devoid of emotion.

It was time to stall for time. "Can't you at least tell us what's going on?"

He raised an eyebrow at me. "You're the one breaking into *their* house, and you want me to explain what's going on to *you*?"

I sighed. At least he was talking, even if he was getting a little upset. I understood it, now. He wanted to remain clinically detached, to treat us like animals or robots rather than people with voices and concerns. That would make it feel too much like murder, I supposed. I decided to double down.

"Why do we have to stand in certain places?" I asked. "If you're just going to kill us—"

He interrupted me. "*We're* not going to kill you, Raven," he said, using my name for the first time. "*They* are." He waved his gun in the general direction of Dan and Laura, who were holding hands in front of the sink. Directing us to stand in certain spots made sense, now. They were orchestrating a murder. A triple murder.

The other man scanned the room a final time and then reached a gloved left hand into a holster hidden behind his back. He produced another handgun that looked to be the same model as the one he was carrying in his right hand. Then, very solemnly, he handed the gun to Dan. A sinking feeling finally settled in my core. They had thought this through. If they pulled it off, it would appear to the police that the three of us had been in a deadly shootout, with no connection to Owen or the church. They would probably make it look like a domestic affair, which would be a snap since one of us was a stripper. The story would almost write itself. Married woman becomes jealous when her husband starts spending time with a stripper. Shots fired. All dead. End of story. "Three Slain in Love Triangle Shootout," the headline would read. Owen would get rid of a pesky witness without leaving any fingerprints. But still, why did Dan and Laura have to die too?

"Now do it," the guy said. "Just like we talked about."

The guy from the Lexus was standing in the doorway, alternating his aim between Dan and Laura and me. They knew they were taking a risk by giving Dan a gun, and I sensed that they were on high alert. Of course, I had no idea what they had planned in advance, but Dan was either going to shoot me or Laura, and then whoever was still alive would be ordered to shoot Dan. We'd all get gunshot residue all over our bodies, of course, which was the whole point. It wasn't the easiest thing in the world to orchestrate, but I could grasp the plan's brilliance.

Not surprisingly, Dan trained his quivering hand towards me. He wasn't my favorite person in the world, but he wasn't a killer, and I could see how grueling this was for him. My heart was racing, eyes darting in every direction seeking a solution, but I was trapped. They'd trained their guns on Dan and me, which I knew would produce similar enough bullet wounds, and I was pinned up against the kitchen table.

Dan did the only sensible thing. He shot at me. But his hand must have been quavering so much that the only damage I sustained was when my eardrums absorbed the booming report. I looked behind me to see a crisp half inch hole in the middle of the wall.

"A good start," the guy in the doorway said wryly. Any gun battle would have more than a few misses, so even Dan's missed shot had been productive. "Now finish it off," he said, waving the gun at Dan.

Dan was sweating now, white faced and still shaking. *I wanted this over with*, I finally admitted to myself. My thoughts had zoomed through all the stages of denial and come to accept my fate. All I wanted was a quick and painless death. Dan leveled the gun at my chest once more. I cringed and closed my eyes.

The shot rang out, piercing the air, and I heard the sickening sound of the bullet ripping through human flesh. And then another shot, and then a third, and when I opened my eyes, the wiry little guy was jumping on Dan's back with his arms around Dan's neck. The guy in the doorway had slumped to the floor, his head making a loud thud as it crashed into the floor. Laura was wide-eyed, pawing ineffectively at the guy on her husband's back. I ran over to the door and tried to wrest the handgun out of a dead man's hand.

His grip on that gun was amazingly tight, and that's when I realized he wasn't dead after all. Despite the pool of inky-red blood underneath him, the guy was powerful enough to flail around onto his stomach, and with all the strength of his core, he turned and pulled, wrenching the gun out of my grip. But I was standing on top of him, and my stripper's legs were strong from years of pole dancing. I began by kicking him in the back of his head. His natural reaction was to cover his head with his hands, but that brought the gun out from underneath him. I began kicking at his gun hand, my bare toes banging into his wrist and fingers until finally he released what I wanted and cowered in a fetal position beneath me. He was losing strength, and fast.

When I reached down to pick up the gun, more shots rang out.

Laura had slumped backwards onto the kitchen table, both hands grabbing her left side where a dark-red stain appeared on her lavender shirt. The gunman was breathing heavily as he surveyed the room. His partner was down and out, he realized, and when he saw me holding his gun, he didn't hesitate. The shot rang out, but not before Dan barreled into the man with all of his two hundred eighty pounds, knocking the man back into the countertop. He still had the gun, though, and trained it directly at Dan.

I squeezed. The man looked confused for a second and realized that the shot had come from me. He grabbed at his chest. I squeezed again, hitting him right at the same spot, driving a hole through the center of his hand. He tried to raise the gun once more, but Dan was all over him now, his nearly three-hundred-pound frame thrusting the bad guy's half-dead body to the floor. The gun slipped away, almost an afterthought.

Dan stood up, huffing and puffing. "He's dead," he said. And then he rushed over to his wife who was looking increasingly pale. He held her head in his hands as she tried to support herself against the table.

A thought occurred to me. "There was just an ambulance across the street," I said. "Maybe they're still there."

I ran out of the kitchen into the living room where the front door was. I never saw it coming.

From my left side, someone jumped on top of me and started pulling wildly at my hair. The blow knocked the wind out of me, and for a moment, I couldn't breathe. It was a sickening feeling, sucking at wind to no effect, barking like a seal all the while. And then it came back gradually, and I pulled at the hands that had made it their business to rip apart my scalp.

They were not strong hands, I realized. The fingers had sharp nails, but they surrendered under my superior strength, and when I had wrested most of them off of my head, I backed myself *hard* into the wall, hoping to crush my assailant behind me. If I had weighed three hundred pounds, it would have worked, but I didn't have enough momentum to make much of a difference. The hands held on. I tried again, harder this time, and I heard a little *thunk* and then a cry. It was an unmistakably feminine cry.

I spun around to see that Dan had arrived, and he was taking us in with utter perplexity. My attacker had backed off for a second, breathing heavily and regrouping, but now she went after me again, a surprisingly strong thrust that pushed me halfway into the kitchen.

"What are *you* doing here?" Dan asked.

"She'll destroy the church!" she shrieked, pointing at me. She had looked familiar to me, but I couldn't quite put it all together until that moment. It was Lisa from one of our card-counting teams. She was the one who'd seemed so *normal*, almost in a June Cleaver sense. Husband, kids, conservative haircut. Now she was looking all over the place, half crazed, and then her eyes focused, and she darted for the countertop and grabbed a scary-looking butcher knife from a wooden knife block stand. She ignored the fact that a woman was dying on the kitchen table. Her focus was exclusively on me.

She lunged at me, and I parried, but she kept herself between me and the other knives in the block. I wondered what Dan had done with the guns, but I couldn't see them anywhere, and Dan didn't seem to have either of them. I shot him a searching look as if to tell him to get his act together, but he seemed dumbfounded by the whole thing. Lisa came at me again, and I barely whirled out of the way, crashing into the countertop in front of the sink. *That one was too close*, I thought. My eyes scanned the room for the guns, but they must have been under the table. Dan kept darting his gaze between the two of us and his wife. Apparently, he was too stressed out to do anything useful to help.

Lisa had me pegged against the counter in front of the sink. I discreetly dropped my left hand behind me to feel around, hoping for a knife or at least a fork, but my fingers promptly landed in a casserole of thick, room temperature goop, which had to be the four-day-old chicken casserole I'd stumbled into on my way in. Lisa was breathing heavily, weighing her next move. She knew that if she lunged for me, Dan would have an opening to either escape or try to tackle her.

I sensed she'd made a decision to come after me, so I was out of time. My right hand reached down into the other sink and fumbled around. No knives. There was a hard, round surface, though, and I snuck a quick peek over my shoulder to see what it was. It had a handle. It would have to do.

She came straight at me, a crazed look in her eyes, the knife held at an ominous angle towards my neck. I tried to stay still, to give her a clear target, like a matador luring a bull straight toward himself, and when she was so close that I could feel her breath, I pulled up with all my strength and hoisted the contents of the saucepan on her, sloshing the disgusting, moldy tomato sauce all across her face and neck a split second before she was at my throat. It didn't stop her.

She plunged the knife right at my throat, but apparently, the sauce had thrown her off enough that she managed only to graze the top of my shoulder. She was on me now with her full weight, smelling rank, a mixture of mold and garlic, pounding at me with her left hand, and trying to reach behind me to stab me in the back with the knife. Her mistake was getting too close.

I tensed my unwholesomely strong leg muscles and then put my full strength behind the knee I leveled into her abdomen. The gasp that escaped her lungs was not unexpected. I had completely knocked the air out of her, and I pressed my advantage by twisting her right arm upwards and then bringing it down, hard, on the countertop. The knife fell out of her hand, sliding into the sink. She was done, I could tell, but I wasn't in the mood to take any chances. I reached down and grabbed the knife and waved it at her.

"Go sit at the table," I ordered. She was still gasping for air, but she managed a small nod of her head and began shuffling over to the table. And that's when things got even worse.

"Drop it," Dan said. He was pointing a gun directly at my throat.

I dropped the knife and gulped.

"We can end this on a positive note," I said, trying to sound rational even though my mind was spinning out of control. Again. Now it was my turn to start breathing heavily.

"It has to be this way, Raven," Dan said almost apologetically.

"Why?" I asked instinctively. Even though a gun was pointed directly at me, I found myself genuinely curious.

"Because it has to," he said unhelpfully.

"All this for the pastor?" I asked, incredulous. "He's a crook, Dan, and I think you know that. He's not worth killing for. And remember, he tried to have *you* murdered too!" This latter point had just popped into my head, and it seemed pretty compelling.

Dan was shaking his head. "You don't understand half of it, Raven." The gun was still pointed at me, but his arm was wavering. Dan was not a killer, I remembered, and I kept thinking of some way to let him drop the gun without losing face. And then it came to me.

"The money," I said matter-of-factly.

He cocked his head slightly. "What money?"

"Owen was paying you off, wasn't he? That's what those five-thousand-dollar wire transfers were every month."

He frowned, seeming angry now. "Who told you about that?"

Lisa, who'd found her way to the table, perked up.

"Your pastor told me," I lied. I didn't want Dan to know I'd been snooping around in his bank account.

Dan slumped, dropping his arm a bit so that the gun was pointed at my abdomen. I didn't think he'd pull the trigger, but I wasn't willing to wager my intestines on it at the moment, so while Dan tried to figure things out, I crouched down and grabbed the knife and hid behind the island.

That proved a mistake.

"Get up!" Dan roared. He couldn't see me, but it would only take him two or three steps to find me. I guessed which way he'd come and then crawled in the opposite direction. It was a lucky guess. I managed to sneak up behind him, and I carved at his leg with the knife, eliciting a surprised shriek of pain from Dan. I jumped up and brought the knife down on his right wrist, causing the gun to slip out. I was much faster than he was, and he was bleeding in two places, so it was no trouble to grab the gun.

I took three or four steps back and surveyed the room. Dan was his usual huffing-and-puffing self, fumbling around at the countertop to find a clean towel. Laura was still pale and was splayed halfway across the kitchen table, but I could see she was still breathing, her eyes following everything that had happened. Lisa, spattered with red sauce, had shrunk into herself. All eyes were on me.

I held the gun on them with my right hand and fished out my phone. Somehow, I managed to dial 9-1-1 with my left thumb. When the dispatcher answered, I said we needed several squad cars and a couple ambulances. And then I hung up.

# CHAPTER TWENTY-EIGHT

———

As a general rule, when the police arrive and find you holding a loaded handgun in a room with two dead bodies, there will be some 'splainin' to do. And probably a little extra if you've somehow managed to come out of the whole thing mostly unscathed.

The police, quite reasonably I thought, believed the explaining should take place at the police station instead of a nasty kitchen full of rotting food. They also, just as reasonably, treated me like a murderer. I didn't even mind when they cuffed me behind my back and led me to the rear of one of the squad cars, where the officer took great care to make sure I didn't bump my head on the way in. I was just happy there were no cameras around. The others met a similar fate, hauled away in separate squad cars. Half the neighborhood had turned out to watch the spectacle.

Fast forward an hour and a half, and the officers had uncuffed me and even provided me with some surprisingly good coffee to soften up the rock-hard muffin I'd politely been picking away at. At first, they were upset that I wasn't confessing, but since I was telling them the kind of story no one would ever make up, they began to soften even more than a week-old muffin dunked in hot coffee.

"Take a look at this," I said, pulling out a piece of paper from my back pocket. I slid it across the table.

"What am I looking at here?" asked the detective in charge, a pudgy bulldog of a man with hangdog jowls and a bald pate that was sorely in need of a fresh shave.

"Every month, these two are getting five grand from a mysterious source. I guessed that it was the Reverend," I said, "and they didn't correct me."

"He's paying them off. But why?" he asked, slurping loudly at his coffee.

"Same as me, I guess. He probably assaulted her, too, but they were willing to be bought off. I wasn't, by the way." I added.

Detective Johansen raised an eyebrow, surveying my disheveled appearance. "I gathered that," he muttered. He was rolling the idea around in his mind. "Husband doesn't work," he muttered. "Needs the money. Makes sense."

"He doesn't work?" I asked.

"Nope. Told us he's been unemployed for a couple years now."

I nodded, chastised. That was something I should have figured out for myself. "No wonder he needed that money," I muttered. "When I accused Owen, I was threatening their steady stream of income."

"I'll take this," he said, picking up the bank statement. "Once you write all this up, you're free to go." He passed me a small typewriter and a stack of forms.

"Should I include this muffin in my report?" I asked innocently.

The junior cop sniffed, stifling a laugh. Johansen fixed him with a *don't encourage her* kind of look. I guessed he had worked with smartass private eyes before, and apparently found it universally distasteful. I winked at the other cop. It would probably get him in trouble, but I'm certain it made his day.

\* \* \*

It was even worse than I'd feared. The hospital told me that Carlos had checked out just hours before I arrived to visit, and when I drove over to his apartment, I knew with one-hundred-percent certainty that *she* was there catering to his every whim and all in all treating him like an overgrown baby. Which is exactly what he needed at the moment.

I hesitated outside, wondering if I should even bother. My appearance would naturally create some stress and might even wake him up, and I didn't want to give her even more ammunition to use against me. But I was there, so I knocked softly at the door.

When the peephole darkened, I swear I could hear a loud, melodramatic sigh through the door. There was a long pause which made me think she wouldn't even open it, but then it opened as far as the chain would allow, and her upset face appeared.

"Go away!" she hissed. "He's not seeing visitors."

I had planned to be as nice as possible, but with her, I just couldn't fake it. "You're not his wife, you know. You don't control who comes and goes. This is *his* house!"

She made some kind of gesture at me with her fingers and cursed in Spanish, and then the door slammed shut. There wasn't anything I could do. Possession is nine-tenths of the law, and there was no denying she had possession of Carlos.

I tried to cheer myself by the fact that he was at home now, which must have meant he was on the mend. But it was no use. Even if he was getting better, he was with *her*. And what made it worse was that I had fallen into the oldest trap in the book. He'd been throwing himself at me for years, and I'd always managed to brush him off. But now that he was with somebody else, I wanted to be with him. Stupid jealousy, that's all it was. Is all life like high school, I wondered?

It was early evening, and I was polishing off some bratwurst and sauerkraut when the phone rang. It was Alex. Rather shyly, he invited me over to his house for dinner.

"We had so much fun the last time," I said, "how could I turn you down?"

He cooked. I protested that I'd already eaten, but it was no use, especially since he'd sautéed two duck breasts and made mushroom risotto which he'd paired with a bottle of pinot noir from Oregon. He wasn't shy about refilling my glass.

"Are you trying to get me drunk?" I asked, hoping the answer was yes.

He held up the bottle which by now was empty. "What do *you* think?"

And then he grabbed my hand and led me down to the basement wine cellar, something I had missed on my first visit. It was a deep vault-like refrigerator set to a cool fifty-five degrees, except instead of being fridge-sized, it was the size of a bedroom. It was stuffed to the gills with almost every slot filled and case after case stacked up on the floor. I wasn't sure if it was the amazing wine or the fact that Alex had a cellar stuffed with amazing wine, but I was getting a fantastic vibe about Alex. He was so intensely pleasant to be with, a man who talked about more than sports, and yet, he also radiated a kind of power that was not attributable only to his wealth. The vibe had been building all evening, but right there in the coolness of the wine cellar, it flooded over me, and at that moment, I knew I needed the warmth of his body against me.

He needed it too. He grabbed me and pulled me close, and then with almost unrestrained abandon, he lifted me up and pressed me against the wall, and after a few minutes of intense passion, he let me down, and we both made our way quickly upstairs to his bedroom.

The next morning, I kissed Alex good-bye and headed out to my car, which was parked in front. Out of the corner of my eye, I noticed movement, and by the time I had spun around, I saw him, camera in hand, snapping my photo. It was the little man the cops had picked up a few nights earlier. The turd. And then I remembered Alex's paranoia, his worry that his wife had hired people to follow him. It all made sense now. The wife was going to get a few choice photos of a fake-boobed floozy leaving her husband's house, and she'd use that as leverage in their divorce proceedings. But that wasn't going to happen on my watch.

I dropped my bag and sprinted at the man, who was taken aback. He paused for a second and then ran into Alex's backyard, which was a mistake. I was wearing my cross-trainers, and I had something inside me that the turd lacked—the knowledge that I was protecting *my man*. I closed on him like a cheetah on a gazelle and then pounced on him, grabbing him around the neck.

The little weasel whined and whinnied. "I'll have you arrested for assault!" he shrieked.

"I'll have you castrated," I said coldly. "I know people."

I wrested the camera out of his hand. "You're trespassing," I said. "Get out of here before I call the police. Again."

By now, Alex had joined us. He was standing there looking menacing, and the turd had no choice but to retreat. He began walking towards the street. "Faster!" I yelled, and he picked up the pace accordingly. We followed and watched him disappear down the road.

I handed the camera over to Alex who took it wordlessly. He was looking at me with a weird expression.

"I saw the whole thing," he said. "I've never seen anything like that before in my whole life. You were amazing."

I shrugged. I supposed it had been pretty dramatic, but in the moment, it seemed the only thing to do.

Alex was looking at the camera, a fancy new DSLR model with a big lens. "I'll bet this thing takes *great* video," he said. Our eyes met.

"You want to come back inside?" Alex asked.

"Yes," I said, smiling. "Yes, I do."

# ABOUT THE AUTHOR

Stephanie Caffrey grew up in Wisconsin and has lived in Chicago, Washington, DC, and London. Although she has traveled the world, her heart belongs to the thumping, degenerate pulse of a city that is Las Vegas. Having stayed at (or passed out in) nearly every casino-hotel on the Strip, she is recognized as an expert on all-things-Vegas, including where to find the best poker rooms, the most decadent foie gras-topped hamburger, and the most effective cure for a tequila-induced hangover. For a brief period in her early twenties, she may or may not have been a topless dancer. A constitutional lawyer by day, she is married with a young son who will not be allowed to visit Las Vegas until he's forty.

To learn more about Stephanie Caffrey, visit her on Facebook at: https://www.facebook.com/stephcaffrey

Enjoyed this book?  Check out these other reads available in print now from Gemma Halliday Publishing:

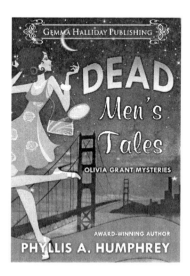

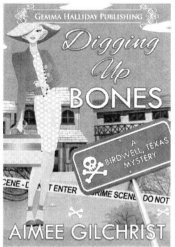

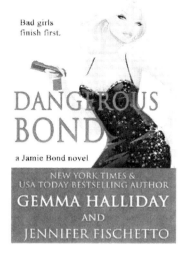

www.GemmaHallidayPublishing.com

CPSIA information can be obtained at www.ICGtesting.com
Printed in the USA
LVOW08s1507060416

482439LV00001B/83/P

9 781530 668311